Camping Canine

Cozy Mysteries with a Dash of Dachshund

Alice Kanaka

This book is a work of fiction. Names, characters, places, and incidents are either the product of the author's imagination or are used ficticiously. Any resemblance to actual persons, living or dead, events, or locales is entirely coincidental.

Table of Contents

Chapter 1 Heading for Adventure .... Page   1
Chapter 2 Salamander .... Page   7
Chapter 3 Fun in the Sun .... Page 15
Chapter 4 Under Cover of Darkness .... Page 23
Chapter 5 Midnight Call .... Page 29
Chapter 6 Easy Money .... Page 35
Chapter 7 Bright New Day .... Page 41
Chapter 8 Don't Leave Town .... Page 47
Chapter 9 Fallout .... Page 53
Chapter 10 Helene Investigates .... Page 59
Chapter 11 The Muddy Boot .... Page 69
Chapter 12 The Seeker .... Page 79
Chapter 13 Mrs. Gross .... Page 89
Chapter 14 Updates .... Page 95
Chapter 15 Arrest .... Page 101
Chapter 16 A Waiting Game .... Page 107
Chapter 17 Leonard to the Rescue .... Page 111
Chapter 18 Modern-day Cowboy .... Page 117
Chapter 19 Assault .... Page 125
Chapter 20 Conference at the Station .... Page 131
Chapter 21 Betrayal .... Page 139
Chapter 22 Darla's Statement .... Page 145
Chapter 23 Leonard's Story .... Page 149
Chapter 24 Unexpected Witnesses .... Page 155
Chapter 25 Marjorie Comes Clean .... Page 159
Chapter 26 Defying Death .... Page 165
Chapter 27 Heard it Through the Grapevine .... Page 171
Chapter 28 Money as a Motive .... Page 177
Chapter 29 He Shot Himself in the Foot .... Page 181
Chapter 30 The Dust Settles .... Page 191
Chapter 31 Dinner Party at Helene's .... Page 197
Chapter 32 Saying Goodbye .... Page 203

More Books by Alice Kanaka

<u>Samantha Olivares Mysteries</u>

The Cardinal & the Crow
The Cardinal, the Fat Boy, & the Flamingo
The Cardinal & the Hawk
The Cardinal & the Crane

<u>Bumfuzzle and Cattywampus: Unlikely Detectives</u>

Trouble at the Buckeye Festival
Mystery at Rutherford Mansion

<u>Mavis & Hornwhistle</u>

Winter Wonderdach
Gallant Guard-dach
Camping Canine

<u>Standalone</u>

Pious Assassin

Chapter 1

Heading for Adventure

Nervous and exhilarated, Lizzy carefully steered the thirty-eight-foot Thor motor coach onto Highway 29. Sitting high above the road, she was captain of her destiny, headed for warm weather and adventure. She glanced at her best friend Holly, who wore an unusually serious expression, and wondered what she was thinking. "Is everything okay?"

"I'm not sure. I mean, it's so much."

"What's so much? Our trip?"

"Just... all of it. The clinic, the RV, you facing your fears. It's a lot to process. This camper is kind of nuts."

"I know, right? I had no idea it was going to be so huge."

Lizzy had rented it online and although there were only two stationary beds, it could comfortably house at least six people. *The full-sized refrigerator and washer and dryer will be convenient. And the fireplace.* "We might as well be comfortable." She paused. "As for the rest, why don't we take a day or two to relax and we'll come up with a plan. The clinic is in good hands. Jason will monitor progress."

"What if..."

"He'll call if there's a problem. This vacation is partly to keep your mind off the construction."

"I know." She looked away, out the window.

When Holly's office burned down, she had been on the verge of giving up her veterinary practice, leading to the impromptu road trip. Something was bothering her, but since Lizzy hadn't figured out what it was, she aimed for distraction.

"I planned some little stops along the way so we can snack and stretch our legs. Mavis will want out too."

"When's the first one?"

"About an hour, but we can stop whenever you want. Check the GPS app for points of interest. Sometimes they don't show up until you get close."

<hr>

Each time they stopped, it was slightly more difficult getting Mavis back in her crate. Lizzy was relieved when they reached their destination, and she could let her miniature dachshund out to run around. The campground near Emporia, Kansas was somewhat remote, but clean and well maintained.

After she parked in their allotted site, Holly stuck her head out the door before retreating back inside. "It's still cold," she complained.

"That's what the fireplace is for. And we can watch movies."

"Two nights, right?"

"Yep. Then we're headed for the tropics." *Not tropics exactly, but Texas is definitely warmer than South Dakota.*

"Aurooherer."

"It's still too early, puppy." Her stomach rumbled and Holly snickered.

"I know, I know. What's for dinner?"

"The pantry's full. What do you want?"

"Pizza." Lizzy laughed. "Just kidding. Sort of. Let's cook on the campfire."

"Do you even know how to make a fire?"

"No. I've never been camping. Do you?"

"Of course. I'll teach you. I saw they're selling wood at the entrance. Let's take our fur babies for a walk."

It was warmer in Emporia, Lizzy guessed around fifty degrees, so she put Mavis' halter on without her winter coat. Holly got Candy into her new miniature harness.

The tiny kitten seemed to think she was a puppy and chased after Mavis, trying to catch her long wagging tail.

Campsites peeked intermittently through the trees along the quiet wooded trail. Lizzy breathed in deeply, reveling in the brisk air, fragranced by wood smoke and pine. "This reminds me of Christmas."

"I never thought of it that way, but I guess you're right. I love the woods."

Their walk took longer than necessary because Mavis had to sniff everything in her path. When they arrived at the lodge, a middle-aged couple sat in rockers on the front porch. *Maybe they're not a couple*, Lizzy thought. *They could be brother and sister.* There was a certain similarity in their round faces, long frizzy hair, and chubby physiques.

Mavis barked and wagged her tail.

The woman smiled and stood. "I saw you come in earlier. What a cute doggy. What's her name?"

"This is Mavis. She's just saying hello."

"What's that?" She pointed at Candy.

"My kitten," Holly said. "She thinks she's a dog."

The woman squinted at Candy. "Make sure you keep them on a leash. Can I help you with anything?"

"We'd like to buy some wood," Holly said.

"Sure. Hank'll carry it back for you. How much do you need?"

"Two bundles, I guess? The RV is self-contained, but it's fun to have a campfire."

"Put it out when you go in for the night."

"We will. Thank you."

Hank carried their wood to the motor home and was more talkative on his own. "Willa's a good woman, but a man can't get a word in. Do either of you do any fishin'?"

"I do sometimes," Holly said. "But not on this trip. Maybe on our way back."

Hank nodded. "Some purdy good fishin' in these parts. Where're you from?"

"Near Sioux Falls."

"Ah. Good fishin' up there too. He nodded again. "Welp. Here we are. I'll leave this here, if that's okay."

"Yes, thank you very much."

He placed the wood near the door then turned to leave, waving with one hand and hitching his trousers up with the other.

Lizzy and Holly glanced at each other and giggled.

"Do we really have to keep Mavis on a leash the whole time we're here?" Lizzy asked.

"I think we'd better. It's in the rules, plus we don't know what kind of wild animals live around here. Too bad we don't have one of those stand-alone pens."

"Let's get one along the way."

Although Holly and her brother had been camping since they could walk, she had never been inside a motor home. It was the best of both worlds, she had to admit. The cookout was fun, but retreating indoors as the temperature dropped was fantastic. The hot shower and comfortable bed, even better. As she closed her eyes, she thought about Lizzy. She had changed a lot, but Holly remembered how traumatized and afraid she had been when she moved to Harperstown a few months earlier. *Lord*, she prayed, *Thank you for Lizzy. Please be with her on this trip.*

At precisely six o'clock, Mavis was up and barking. Lizzy had taken the master bedroom with the door so she wouldn't have to carry the dog up and down the ladder. Holly lay on the loft bed above the cab and opened her eyes. *I should get up.* Warm and comfortable, she didn't want to move. The door clicked shut and wrapped in stillness, her eyes closed.

The next time she woke, the motor home was quiet. She tried to sit up and banged her head before remembering where she was. *Oww.* She flopped on her back and rubbed the sore spot. Mavis' medium-pitched barking sounded far away and was answered by Lizzy's unintelligible murmur. With a wide yawn and a long stretch, Candy jumped on Holly's mass of tangled hair. "I guess it's time to get up, huh? I wonder what time it is."

When she finally went outside, she was shocked. Not only had Lizzy built a fire by herself, but she was also cooking bacon and pancakes.

"What? When did you learn how to make pancakes?"

Mavis danced on her hind legs. "Ahrooherer," she said, in her own special language.

Sporting a hilarious bedhead, Lizzy stood by the campfire wielding a spatula. "Right now. I found a recipe in that cookbook you gave me."

"I'm… Let's just say I'm very impressed."

"I don't know how they'll taste. I might have burned a few. Mavis didn't mind though. Did you girl?"

"Roherer."

"Are you hungry?"

"Starved. What time is it?"

"It's only eight. Mavis woke me up early."

"I know. I heard. Sorry I didn't get up."

With a slight lift of her brows, Lizzy said, "It's not your job to take my silly puppy outside at the break of dawn. Besides, you barely sleep at all."

"You know, I've never thought about it, but I always sleep better when I'm camping. Maybe it's the fresh air or the extra exercise."

"Whatever it is, take advantage of it. Don't go jumping out of bed when you don't have to. Want some coffee?" She retrieved a percolator pot from the grill and poured two cups.

"You're really embracing this camping thing.

"Next you'll be wanting to sleep in a tent."

"I set one up on the bed," Lizzy said. Then she laughed at Holly's expression. "I didn't, but I'd like to try it sometime. Outdoors, not on the bed."

"Don't worry. We go tent camping every summer."

"Who? Your family?"

"Sometimes, or with friends. You'll see. Pass me that cup."

Chapter 2

Salamander

Salamander Elkhurst had far-reaching dreams. He sat in the campground check-in window perusing celebrity magazines. His job didn't pay much, enough to buy camera equipment if he saved, but it left him plenty of time to study famous faces and build his portfolio.

The mostly solitary nature of the work suited him. For the majority of his twenty-five years, he had been mocked and ridiculed by his peers. His unusual face, the kinky orange hair, and the name his mother had gifted him with. *What had she been thinking?* For as long as he could remember, the other kids called him Sally.

Sometimes his friend Patricia drove her dilapidated Ford Escort to the campground, and they'd take a short hike. Insects were her passion and after studying Entomology at the university, she spent most of her time on research.

That afternoon, she had arrived with snacks and new magazines from her mother's beauty salon. "Can you take a break?" she asked. "I need to clear my head."

"Yeah, hold on a sec." He told his boss he'd be gone for half an hour and do a walk-around inspection while he was out. He grabbed his camera and left.

They moved slowly through the woods, Patricia crawling through the bushes and enthusiastically calling him over to take pictures of unusual insects. Her ardor and dedication mirrored his own. He took close-up photos of small flowers and wildlife, and sometimes Patricia.

She wasn't beautiful, although Salamander suspected she could be.

Her mousey brown hair and unfortunately prominent ears led to her nickname, Mickey. She was an outsider like him, and they bonded over the bullying they endured.

Standing with a grin, she brushed the dirt off her knees and adjusted her thick glasses. "I suppose you have to get back."

"I probably should."

"Thanks for this." She spread her arms. "It was exactly what I needed."

"You know I always enjoy hunting bugs with you."

Patricia laughed. "I know I get a little carried away."

They walked back to the wooden structure that housed the check-in window, a small gift shop on one side and the managers' living quarters on the other. Sal hugged her and said, "Thanks for coming by and for the magazines. One of these days I'm going to get my big break. You'll see."

"I know you will. Even if you don't become a world-renowned paparazzi, your photographs are stunning. They'll end up in a museum somewhere and people will pay thousands to buy them."

He grinned and waved as she walked back to her car.

After his shift, he rode his dirt bike home and tried to sneak upstairs, but his father caught sight of him as he passed the living room.

"Get cleaned up. Your mother made pot roast."

He sighed. They knew he hated roast beef. "How long?"

"Half an hour."

He trudged up the stairs. He needed a shower anyway.

Sitting with his parents at the dinner table, he kept his head down and his mouth shut. That didn't work.

"Your mother and I have been talking. It's time you began contributing to the household. You can go to college or get a job but you're too old to be living at home and doing nothing."

"But…"

"No buts. Decide what you want to do and start making plans."

Sal lowered his eyes but inside he was fuming. *All I need is one huge score. Then I can move out.*

"Dessert dear?" his mother asked sweetly.

———————✖︎———————

The second day in Emporia flew by. One day to break up the trip and acclimate to the RV. As they hiked around the small campground and cooked over the fire, Lizzy was amused by the novelty of being outdoors but anxious to reach warmer weather. The next morning when she and Holly rose early and prepared to continue their journey, she was full of energy. It was Holly's turn to drive and as she became accustomed to their oversized vehicle, her muscles gradually unclenched and her unnaturally high-pitched voice lowered to its normal range. "It's quite comfortable, isn't it?"

Lizzy nodded. "Not as hard as it looks."

"I wanted to tell you, you were right. About taking a couple of days to relax. I feel better now."

"I'm glad. You've been through a lot."

"Now it's your turn. I'm worried about you. What if someone recognizes you and you end up in the news again?"

"It'll be okay. You'll see. Anyway, we have three nights at the next place to plan."

"You're in charge of the rest stops this time so you'd better get busy."

"I've already picked out the first one."

"I like our short travel days," Holly said. "When we go camping with Dad, we always arrive late and have to set up camp in the dark."

"Six hours still feels like a long time, even with all the breaks. I'm glad we'll be able to stay for a while."

"Did you say they have a pool?"

"That's what it says on the website."

"I wonder if it'll be warm enough to swim."

"It's supposed to be heated. Cross your fingers."

Kindred souls. Salamander observed Emiliano and his wife Brielle preparing to open for the day. *They're different, just like me.* The campground managers were two of the few people he liked in town. He guessed they were a little older than he was, and that they had their own reasons for hiding out in the backwoods.

"Can you check the guests in today?" Brielle asked. "Emiliano has to repair one of the showers and I wanted to get a head start on the garden."

"No problem." He grinned. *More time for me to read the celebrity news.* On his breaks, when Patricia didn't visit, he wandered the trails. He knew the forest better than anyone, even Emiliano.

At lunch time, Brielle brought him something to eat. She often cooked to suit her husband's taste and that day she prepared a ham torta, piled high with fresh vegetables and peppers. Salamander ate at a leisurely pace, relishing the crisp and savory combination. When he was finished, he carefully wiped his neat goatee and tucked the paper plate into a small garbage can at his feet, then looked up at the sound of an approaching vehicle. A motor home pulled up at the check-in gate and the driver descended from the cab. Sal's pulse quickened as she rounded the front. *Can it be?* His research had finally paid off. *A real-life celebrity: one who disappeared three months ago.* He was almost afraid to believe his good luck. Yet there she was, Elizabeth Hornwhistle, her unmistakable waist-length brown hair blowing in the light breeze.

"Hello." Her red lips smiled in greeting. "I have a reservation for Lizzy Horn."

Chuckling to himself, he logged into the computer. *Not too creative as aliases go. She seems friendly.*

His fingers itched to pick up his camera. *Don't blow it. This is your chance. Just play it cool.* Her reservation was near the entrance, but he swapped it for a site deeper in the woods. "Make sure to hang this on your rear-view mirror during your stay. And this map might come in handy if you do any hiking." His hand touched hers and he shivered.

After he checked her in, he watched her resume the driver's seat in the enormous RV and wondered if she was traveling alone. The rig was roomy enough for a family, but celebrities were funny. *If she's living in it, like a house, she might just like her space. I'll find out.* It occurred to him that an interview would make the photos even more valuable. *But the news said she disappeared, so she probably doesn't want to be found. I wonder why. Perhaps she'd pay to keep her secret.* He turned the idea over in his mind but decided keeping her secret wouldn't help advance his career; the career that would get him out of his parents' house and shut them up once and for all.

⊷∙⊸⫘⊶∙⊷

Holly climbed back into the driver's seat and frowned. The man who checked her in was off somehow. He had very short red hair and a sharp goatee of the same color, slightly bulging brown eyes and a small mouth; an odd combination. But it wasn't his appearance that made her uncomfortable, it was his intense scrutiny. He smiled, but his eyes were calculating.

"Did you see that guy who checked us in?"

"No, sorry," Lizzy said from the back. "Was he good looking?"

"No. He was kind of creepy." Holly shivered.

"Creepy scary?"

"I'm not sure. It was probably my imagination." She didn't say anything more, but the look in his eyes lingered in her mind.

The campground was located deep in the forest, with plenty of room between campsites. Lizzy moved to the passenger seat. "We should back into our spot so it's easier to pull out when we leave."

"You do it. I'm afraid I'll hit something. Where are the hookups?"

"I don't know. I guess that could make a difference."

When Holly stopped in front of site number forty-eight, she opened the door and climbed down. She flung her arms out and spun in a circle, her face raised toward the sun. "It's gorgeous here. Warm too. I love it!"

Located at an intersection, the spacious campsite sat nestled among trees and bushes that shielded it from the dust and noise of the road. Lizzy got out and surveyed the site. "Perfect. The hookups are in the back. We should have asked where they're hiding the pool."

"That guy at the entrance gave me a map."

Lizzy moved to the driver's seat and backed neatly between two trees before making her way into the rear to release her wiener dog.

Mavis somehow knew they had reached their destination. She pranced happily, barking and jumping on Lizzy's leg.

"I'll make sandwiches," Holly said, "then we can go for a hike."

"What about the pool?"

"Study the map while I throw lunch together."

"I wish we had some kind of small vehicle we could drive into town."

"Not having one could be saving us from ourselves. Otherwise, we might spend all our time shopping."

"There is that."

Armed with sandwiches and towels, they walked down the long path to the road, taking a right and rounding the corner. Sunny and in the mid-seventies, the weather felt like summer. Mavis leapt over roots and wound her leash around slender saplings, Candy on her tail. Deciduous trees, turning green as they sprouted new growth, filtered the blue sky and the bright sunlight on either side of the gravel road.

The first three sites on the left apparently belonged to an extended group. Multiple tents in a variety of sizes, shapes, and colors dotted the area and picnic tables were pushed together.

Catchy dance music blared, *Minelli*, Lizzy thought, and she wondered if the noise would bother them at night. Half a dozen young people moved about the site, pitching tents, dancing, and hollering over the music. Mavis barked and wagged her tail.

One of the campers beckoned them, raising her voice to be heard. "Hi! I'm Freida. You're in the rig around the corner right?"

Lizzy nodded.

"We're having a party tonight. B.Y.O.B. Come on over if you want."

"Thanks. We might take you up on that."

Freida turned her head when someone yelled her name. "Sorry. I've gotta go. See you tonight."

Once they were out of earshot, Holly asked, "How old do you think they are? Are they legal?"

"I'd guess early twenties, so some of them."

Holly tripped on a root and fell. "Ow." She sat back and examined the scrapes on her knees.

"Are you okay?" Lizzy reached down to help her up.

"I'm fine. I saw something shiny and wasn't paying attention to my feet."

"Ooh shiny." Lizzy chuckled.

"No, seriously. The sun reflected off something. I think someone's watching us."

"Well, you *are* stunning but we're also in the middle of the woods, so not super likely."

Holly brushed the dirt off and giggled. "That's not what I meant."

They walked past several vacant sites, stopping to stare at an eighties-style fifth wheel on the right, rocking back and forth as if possessed. "Somebody's having a good time."

Clothes hung on a rope tied between two trees and an old Jeep was parked around the back.

"Maybe we're having an earthquake and just didn't notice."

Holly's giggling stopped suddenly. "Look. There it is again."

"What?"

"That reflected light I saw before. Let's go check it out." She pointed toward a thick stand of bur oaks.

"I don't know. We're almost at the pool."

Tilting her head, Holly frowned.

"We don't know who or what it is. Next time we'll bring something to protect ourselves and we can investigate, okay?"

"You think they might be dangerous?"

"I have no idea but consider what items might reflect sunlight. It could be binoculars or someone setting up a tent, but it could also be a weapon." *I should have brought the TASER. I didn't realize it would be so deserted out here.* She wasn't too worried, but didn't want to take any unnecessary risks with Holly along.

Chapter 3

Fun in the Sun

Sal took a break and offered to work late. He strolled down to Elizabeth's campsite, then slid behind a coppice of trees to observe. He didn't recognize the tall blonde woman. *Probably a friend or a relative.* He caressed his camera. She could be famous too. Dressed in shorts and T-shirts, they carried backpacks and had two pets, a yappy dog and a small white ball of fluff. He thought it might be a cat, but that would be weird. *The summer clothes are kind of strange too, but maybe they're from somewhere cold.*

Trailing them silently through the woods, he quickly ducked behind a cedar elm. Elizabeth was very observant. She almost caught him twice. But he got a handful of good photos. Then he chuckled when Freida invited them to the big keg party. *Another great photo-op.*

He hated Freida. In high school, she got around, but Salamander was willing to overlook that when she asked him to their senior Prom. She led him on until the day of the event, then laughed with her friends when she publicly humiliated him. He could still hear her words. "I can't believe you'd think I would actually go to Prom with a loser like you." *At least I don't have to make other people feel small to feel good about myself.*

He was about to turn back when he realized Elizabeth and her friend were going to the pool. *They'll be disappointed.* The website advertised a heated pool, but the heater had been broken for years. *At least it's clean.*

Elizabeth opened the gate and held it for the blonde. She squatted down and stuck her hand in the water. "I don't think it's heated."

"Is it warm enough to get in?" Her friend unclipped her dog's leash.

"The question is, can we warm up once we get out?"

"Mavis!" The blonde woman dove in after the little dog.

Elizabeth stood by the edge of the pool and laughed. Sal took pictures, one after the other. She was so beautiful.

When her friend surfaced, she giggled. "Mavis loves to swim. I forgot to tell you."

"I can't believe you. Get in here right now."

"Yes, ma'am." Elizabeth giggled again and removed her shorts and T-shirt. Unlike her friend, treading water in soggy clothes, she was a forties pinup girl in a modest red one-piece, her long dark hair piled on top of her head. Sal continued to shoot. *These photos will be gold.*

He knew he should be getting back to work, but he lingered, afraid to miss anything. He watched the young ladies splash and play with the dog, who swam circles around them. He heard a meow from the white ball of fluff and noticed it didn't get in the water with the others. *Brielle would have a fit if she saw the dog in there.*

They finally got out. He took pictures of Elizabeth drying off, then returned to his post, excitedly imagining his future fame.

⊷⧒⊶

After hanging her outer clothes to dry in the sun, Lizzy lay face down on a recliner and shivered. "It might be a little chilly yet for that."

"It was so refreshing though. Just what I needed." Holly, face up, contemplated her kitten. "Poor Candy. I wish she could have joined us."

Lizzy turned over. "Where are those sandwiches?"

"In my bag."

"Give me a minute and I'll get them. The sun feels so good."

"It's hot. I could go back in now."

"Let's wait until tomorrow. As soon as we're in the shade it'll feel cold, and my clothes are soaked."

"Yeah. I guess so, but Mavis doesn't agree."

Mavis pulled at her leash and whined.

"She got me in. Little stinker. I thought she was going to drown."

"I totally forgot. My mom told me about how much she loves water. Mom said she tried to dive off a waterfall once and was dangling mid-air by her harness."

Holly's mother had been Mavis' temporary caregiver after her previous owner died, and before she adopted Lizzy. She followed an intruder into her new house and decided to stay.

Having retrieved the backpack, Lizzy searched through it for their lunch. "It's so interesting seeing what you bring along on our little excursions."

"I find your choices interesting as well," Holly said. "Mostly unexpected."

"It might be fun to play show and tell sometime and explain what we brought and why."

"We should make a rainy-day list."

"What do we have *here*?" Lizzy asked as she unwrapped a sandwich and gave it a sniff.

"Roast beef, provolone, and horseradish mustard."

"Mm. I wonder if Mavis likes horseradish."

"She likes everything."

"That's true. She even ate a jalapeno once. I'm not sure if she actually has taste buds."

"Is there anything she won't eat?"

"Lemons. She tries, but she just can't."

Taking a bite of her sandwich, Lizzy declared it delicious, and when she dropped a piece, Mavis added her approval.

"You're getting pink already," she told Holly. "How did you remain Snow White after two weeks in Florida?"

"Heavy applications of sunscreen and a hat. I wasn't thinking about it today. It snuck up on me."

"You ready to head back?"

"I guess we should. It's so lovely and warm, I feel like taking a nap."

"Let's save something for tomorrow."

As they hiked back to their campsite, Lizzy noticed many of the previously vacant spots were occupied and smoke rose from campfires along the way. Mavis barked at everything, seen and unseen. Candy began to tire, so Holly let her ride on her shoulder.

"I think I'll cook inside tonight, if that's okay."

"Why?"

"It's just a lot easier. We can still have a campfire and eat outside if you want."

"Aurooherer."

"Uh oh. Someone heard the magic word."

"You can set up her new pen and the hammock, then give her some d-i-n-n-e-r while I cook."

"Is it too early? We just ate."

"I don't know about you, but all this exercise makes me hungry."

"Roherer." Mavis' tail increased in speed.

"Shoot. Too smart for her own good."

<hr>

By the time Lizzy showered and changed, fed Mavis, hung the new hammock, made the fire, and set up the pen, she really *was* hungry. The scent of Holly's cooking wafted through the window, making her stomach grumble.

"Inside or out?" Holly called.

"I'll come in. What's on the menu? It smells great."

"Rice, rosemary-lemon chicken, and steamed peas and carrots."

"I might be drooling a little." Lizzy entered the RV and sat at the fold-out table. Holly carried two plates to the table and joined her.

Mavis moaned and whined dramatically.

"If I hadn't fed her myself, I'd think she was starving."

"She's a good little actress."

"I don't know how you can make something so delicious so fast," Lizzy said, changing the subject.

"I told you before; this type of meal is super easy. Next time I'll let you do it, so you'll know how."

The chicken was moist, with exactly the right amount of seasoning. "It's like restaurant food."

"I just pan-fried frozen tenders with salt, pepper, and rosemary leaves, then when they were browned, I squirted some lemon juice on them and put the lid on, so it didn't splatter all over the place."

"These are rosemary? They don't look like leaves." Lizzy scooped a few of the browned sticks with her fork. "I like them."

"Me too. Jason doesn't though."

Why did she bring him up? She pictured Holly's brother in her mind, tall and slender with serious green eyes. "Do you miss him?"

"What? No. It's only been three days. I just thought of him because he's the only one who's ever complained about my cooking."

"Next time you can tell him he's just plain wrong. Your cooking is the best."

"You're just saying that, so I'll cook for you."

"Noo. It really is the best. But please keep cooking for me."

Holly giggled. "As long as you help with the dishes."

"I think you already did most of them."

"Who knew you could get a camper with a dishwasher? In fact, I've changed my mind. I'll finish up in here and you take Mavis out and show her the pen."

"Deal."

Mavis wasn't thrilled with her enclosure.

She'd rather be free to explore. But she settled in once Lizzy added her bed and a new rawhide bone.

<hr>

Holly carried Candy outside, placing her in the pen with Mavis, and handed Lizzy a beer. The sun began to set and the air cooled but compared to South Dakota it felt like summer. She sank into her canvas folding chair and sighed. It had been a long day.

"Your hair is glowing pink and orange."

"Really? That sounds kind of cool. Take a picture so I can see it."

"My phone's inside. Hand me yours." She almost missed it. "It's not the same as before," she said, as she returned the phone.

Lizzy studied the photo and grinned. "You'll have to be quicker next time."

"I've been wondering about your plan once we get to L.A. Are you planning on using me as a double?" Before Lizzy had cut and bleached her hair and dropped twenty pounds, she had appeared much like Holly. She had also altered the way she dressed and lightened her makeup, making herself virtually unrecognizable.

"No, in fact we'll have to make sure we're not seen together at the conference. And that you're not seen with Mavis."

"If someone takes your picture, will they be able to find you again?"

"They'll at least be able to follow me. I have a wig and different clothes for my public appearances. Kirk said he'll help."

Kirkland Schwartz, Lizzy's attorney and trusted friend, had helped her escape her sudden fame and arranged her speaking engagement in Los Angeles.

Lizzy canted her head and squinted at Holly. "Could you wear a hat or a bun and change your makeup a little, so no one mistakes you for me?"

"This is starting to sound fun; like being a super spy, infiltrating the publishing world."

"Stop." Lizzy chuckled. "You're beginning to think like me."

Mavis stood and cocked an ear. Then, barking, she ran to one side of the pen and stared into the shadows behind the RV.

A man and a woman emerged from the trees and approached the campfire.

"There you are," said the man. He was gaunt, all elbows and knees, with a small mustache and angry-looking acne. "We came to walk you to the party. You're still coming, right?"

Lizzy shrugged. "I suppose we can go for a bit. We don't have much to drink on board," she fibbed. "Just a few beers."

"No biggie. We have plenty. Cool dog."

Mavis barked like a poo-bah and wagged her tail.

"Give us a minute to lock up." Holly said.

"Sure. I'm Freida, in case you forgot. This is my boyfriend Jim."

Freida was as tall as Lizzy, perhaps five-ten, with stringy brown hair, a prominent nose, and very thin lips. She reminded Holly of a giraffe.

"Good to see you again. Just a sec."

Holly went inside to help with the pets.

"Bring a sweater and a flashlight." Lizzy put her camping knife in one pocket and a TASER in the other.

At least she's not bringing her gun.

They left Mavis outside her crate and turned on the security system before locking the door. Lizzy doused the campfire with a bucket of water, and they followed Freida and Jim back through the trees to their campsite.

The forest floor was ink, thick branches blotting out the moon and stars. The party site glowed in the distance, throwing the path into ever darker shadows. Fairy lights, tiki torches, and a roaring campfire must have served as beacons for the burgeoning crowd, Lizzy thought. *Surely there weren't this many people here this afternoon.*

Freida poured them beers from one of several kegs and yelled introductions over the blaring music. Then she vanished into the darkness.

Chapter 4

Under Cover of Darkness

At dusk, Sal camouflaged his dirt bike in some bushes before setting off on foot. Carrying a bottle of water and assorted camera equipment in his backpack, he slinked silently through the underbrush, stopping occasionally to listen for unwelcome company. He looped around the campsite, hunting for locations with good visibility and adequate concealment. He experimented with the night settings on his camera as he went, and practiced taking shots from various angles and distances, until he was confident he could take advantage of any situation.

Scouting a good location across the road, he set up his tripod and watched as darkness fell. The number of partygoers multiplied, as did the volume, the bright light and music masking his presence. Bored and wishing he had a chair; he told himself to be patient and pulled out his water.

There they are! He thanked the universe for his luck when Elizabeth and her friend crossed the road behind Jim and Freida. Elizabeth was beautiful, as always, even in plain slacks and a cardigan. *It's too bad she's just like the others.* He took picture after picture, documenting their attendance at the local beer bash. *It would be so amazing if I could get a shot of her doing something illegal or running away when the police get here.* He considered making an anonymous call to help things along but decided to wait.

———————

At first, Lizzy and Holly were occupied with questions and small talk, mainly from the young men in attendance.

They circled, vying for attention from the two women from out of town. Lizzy was twenty-eight and Holly thirty, although she looked younger. *Hey, I'm Kyle… Do you like football?… Are you from around here?… Mark's the quarterback… Want another drink?*

The women—girls?— weren't as friendly, either whispering amongst themselves or flirting with intention.

Lizzy stood very still, absorbing everything around her. On the surface, it was just another teen keg party, but she sensed something else going on. A few of the guests were older, for one thing. A lone man sat by the fire, occasionally joined by one or two party-goers, who conferred briefly before making a surreptitious exchange.

Like a wraith, Freida appeared beside them. "There's someone I'd like you to meet. Come on." She tugged on Lizzy's sleeve.

Lizzy raised her eyebrows in question and Holly shrugged.

Lit from within, the eight-person tent was pitched facing the woods, the entrance in shadow. Freida unzipped the flap and said, "We're here."

Curious, Lizzy crawled in after her, leaving Holly to enter last. Once inside, she rose to her feet and glanced around. A woman with a black bob sat in a lotus position on an air mattress in the center of the tent. When she stood, the tent felt smaller. Her Junoesque figure and her strong square facial features left an unforgettable impression that caused Lizzy's fingers to itch. She needed to write.

Frieda introduced them to Mary.

Stretching out her hand in greeting, she said, "How do you do?" in a deep, velvety voice.

Goosebumps. What a voice.

"Come. Sit with me and tell me all about your travels," Mary said. She managed to drive a lively, entertaining conversation without divulging anything personal.

But Lizzy was curious. "Why are you in here instead of joining the party?" she asked.

Freida jumped in. "Mary's a sort of celebrity. She's here with her husband but doesn't want too much attention."

"Talking to you is refreshing," Mary said. "I'd love to travel around in a giant RV like you're doing. It sounds very exciting."

"I've never been anywhere," Freida complained.

"It's easy to get stuck in a rut, isn't it? And having to keep a low profile makes it worse. Sometimes I wish…"

The man from the campfire poked his head into the tent. "Could we talk for a minute?" he asked Mary.

"Of course. It was great meeting you two. Perhaps we can visit again some time."

"That would be lovely," Lizzy agreed.

Outside the tent, Freida once again left them to fend for themselves. They wandered around, mostly ignored, finally sitting by the fire.

"She was mesmerizing," Holly said.

"Puzzling. I have so many questions, but the answers are incidental. Whatever I can make up is probably more interesting than the true story."

"I feel uncomfortable, like people are staring," Holly whispered. "What if that guy comes back?"

"Okay. Let's make our escape."

They stood and gradually moved toward the road, trying not to be obvious. Lizzy could feel eyes following them until they left the bright light of the party and the darkness of the periphery engulfed them. She switched on their flashlight once they reached the road but had to jump back into the bushes when two pickups raced by, hoots and hollers sounding from the truck beds as more guests headed for the party.

Lizzy closed her eyes momentarily, letting her breathing slow.

"Lizzy?"

"Yes?"

"Could you let go of my arm? It hurts a little."

Her eyes flew open, and her head turned toward her friend. "Oh my gosh. I'm sorry." She released her vice grip on Holly's upper arm. "Are you okay?"

"I'm fine. I was just starting to lose circulation."

They continued their walk home and blinked when the motor home's blinding security lights flashed on.

"Nice timing," Holly said.

"I suppose it depends on how you look at it." Several silhouetted figures raced into the trees. Mavis' frantic barking sounded from inside. She calmly unlocked the door and picked her up.

"Good puppy," she said in a soothing voice, stroking her ears.

"What was that?"

"I think we should call the police."

"But… were they trying to break in?"

"We can watch the security footage first, if you want, but I suspect they invited us to the party so we wouldn't be here."

Holly's lips formed an *O*. "Do you really think so?" At Lizzy's nod, she said, "Call first and we can watch while we wait."

Lizzy called 911 and reported an attempted break in, then sat with Holly and backed the recording to the beginning. She held Mavis and watched as Jim and two other young men rounded the RV, checking the doors and windows. Mavis barked along with the recording. When it was finished, Lizzy set it back to record and contemplated what she'd seen. There was someone in the trees, watching. The security lights had glinted off something; perhaps the same thing Holly had noticed that afternoon. *A camera? Should I mention it to her? She's already spooked.*

—•◦⟨⟩◦•—

They're leaving. I was wrong. She's not like all the rest. Sal stuffed his belongings into his backpack and took a shortcut to Elizabeth's campsite. In time to see Jim and his pals approach the camper, he circled to a spot where he could see them and raised his camera.

The security lights blinked on and one of the men glanced in Sal's direction. He punched Jim in the arm. "Someone's over there. Let's scram."

Running for the trees, they didn't see Elizabeth and her friend arrive. *What would they have done if they'd been confronted?* Sal clenched his fingers around his camera. He wandered the area for a while, taking random pictures, but finally lost interest, returning to where he had left his dirt bike and heading home.

Although not opposed to digital cameras, that night he had used proper film with two detachable lenses: a fifty millimeter and a twenty-eight. He developed the film himself in his bathroom-turned-darkroom and discovered more than he expected. He mulled over his bonanza as he fell across his bed. Despite his exhaustion, he was unable to sleep. He lay for hours considering his most profitable course of action. *This must be what the pros face every day. But I don't have time to shop around. I need cash.*

Chapter 5

Midnight Call

After two hours, they gave up. "Let's just go to bed. I don't think they're coming," Lizzy said.

"It's strange, isn't it? Even with only three officers, I've never had to wait this long for the police to respond in Harperstown. This town can't be much bigger. Can it?"

Lizzy shook her head. It occurred to her that Holly had special treatment since the captain was her brother, but still, two hours was excessive. She stood and called Mavis, "Come on, girl. Potty time."

The little dog ran to the door, then promptly rolled onto her back when Lizzy tried to put her harness on. "You're such a little stinker. At least we don't have to deal with your coat." She clipped on the leash and opened the door. "Be right back."

She had to admit she was a little nervous going outside by herself, but Mavis had sharp ears and would bark if anyone was around. She even barked at the wind. The security lights helped too, dispelling the shadows around the motor home.

Holly opened the door. "Are you okay out there by yourself?"

"Of course. I have my guard-dach with me."

Nodding skeptically, Holly retreated into the relative safety of the RV.

Once Mavis finished her business, Lizzy took her back inside and headed for the bedroom.

"Goodnight," Holly called from the loft. "See you in the morning."

"Okay. Sleep well."

Lizzy washed her face and put on her pajamas, then sat on the edge of the bed, where Mavis was jumping around like a rabbit. "I would think you'd be worn out after all the hiking and swimming. Why do you have so much energy all of a sudden?"

Mavis barked once and wagged her tail.

"Hm. It's bedtime now. Do you think we can sleep a little?" She rose and pulled her bedspread back and before she could climb in, Mavis had burrowed to the foot of the bed.

Tossing and turning, Lizzy finally drifted off to sleep. She groaned when Mavis woke her with insistent barking. The security lights blinked on, and someone banged on the door. Lizzy rolled out of bed and followed Mavis out of the bedroom in time to see Holly pulling on her housecoat on her way to the door.

"Who is it?" she asked.

Lizzy couldn't hear the answer over the barking. She shook her head at the way Mavis' loud, medium-pitched bark somehow sounded like three or four dogs instead of one.

When Holly opened the door, two uniformed policemen stood at the bottom of the steps. "I'm Corporal Quirk and this is Officer Garcia. You reported an attempted break in?"

"What time is it?" Lizzy rubbed her eyes and squinted at her phone. "You might as well have waited until morning. We called three hours ago."

"We can just leave if you don't need assistance." Corporal Quirk, about Lizzy's height and soft, sounded condescending. He shifted his weight from one foot to the other and rattled his keys.

His subordinate frowned faintly. "I apologize for our late visit. Would you rather we come back?"

"No, we're up now. Come on in." Lizzy picked Mavis up and shushed her. "Would you like some coffee?"

"Yes, please," Garcia said. He glanced around the motor home. "This is really nice."

"It's a rental."

Mavis had settled down, so Lizzy invited them to sit and started a pot of coffee.

"Are you from around here?"

"No, we're on a road trip."

"Why don't we get down to business?" Quirk asked. He shook his keys again, prompting Mavis to resume her barking. "Can't you shut that dog up?"

"If you'd stop messing with your keys, she'd stop barking."

Garcia tried to hide his smile.

Holly joined her at the counter. "I'll finish this. Go ahead and show them the footage."

"Thanks." Lizzy moved toward the security system control panel. A flat screen monitor slid from its compartment and with the push of several buttons, she started the recording.

The police officers watched carefully as Jim and two other men circled the RV.

"There's no doubt what they were up to," Officer Garcia said. He accepted a cup of coffee from Holly.

"What do you reckon spooked them?" Quirk asked. "They didn't pay no mind to the dog or the lights."

"Can you go back just a bit?"

Lizzy backed the recording to just before the men ran.

"There. Pause." Garcia leaned forward. "Something in the trees."

"Like when we were hiking," Holly said.

"You reckon Sally was out there?" Quirk started to rattle his keys but glanced at Mavis and stopped. She wagged her tail.

"Who's Sally?" Lizzy asked.

"Our wannabe papa-rotsee. He's gonna get himself in trouble one of these days."

Garcia looked thoughtful. "Let's get this form filled out and we'll take it from here." He slid a stack of papers across the table. "Go ahead and fill in your personal information. There's not much we can do, since they didn't actually break in, but we can have a word with them."

Lizzy liked Officer Garcia. She wasn't so sure about Quirk. He reminded her of Nettle, that stupid lazy deputy back home. Except this version of Nettle was in charge.

Once they were finished with the paperwork, they shook hands and said goodnight. Lizzy locked the door behind the officers and asked, "Where'd we put the Malibu?"

"I think it's in the fridge."

"You up for a cocktail?"

Holly nodded. "What did you think of those two?"

"Complete opposites. Quirk remind you of anyone?"

"Charlie Brown?" She giggled.

Lizzy paused. "I didn't think of that. The glasses kind of ruin the effect."

"I didn't even notice them."

"That's probably because they were frameless, except for the solid frame across the top."

"Who did he remind you of?"

"Nettle."

"Personality, you meant. His partner seems a lot nicer. Cuter too." Holly smiled.

"They do the good cop/bad cop schtick very well. Do you suppose that's on purpose?"

"Probably not. Do you think we can check out early? I don't feel safe here anymore."

"We can do whatever we want. It's our vacation." Lizzy grinned and handed Holly a glass of Malibu and orange juice.

<hr>

After unsuccessfully trying to sleep for several hours, Sal finally texted Patricia. 'Can I come over?'

'Yes. Come now.'

Sal smiled and snuck down the stairs to avoid a confrontation with either of his parents.

She was waiting for him and led him upstairs to her room. "Want a snack?" she asked.

Cross-legged on the floor, he asked, "What've you got?"

"Jerky or cashews?"

"Jerky sounds good."

Grabbing an unopened bag off her desk, she sat across from him and tossed him the bag. "So, what's up?" She removed her glasses and rubbed the bridge of her nose.

"You look beat. Are you getting enough sleep?"

She smiled. "You're the only one who ever notices. Tell me why this late-night visit."

"Something's happened and I need a favor." He told her about the party and his photos. "I'm going to leave most of them with Helene, but I don't want to involve her with this one. Will you keep it for me?"

Patricia scrutinized the picture. "I'll do whatever you ask, but this is serious. Think it through carefully before you do anything."

"I will."

"Do you want to stay over?"

"No, not tonight, but thanks for being here for me. I'll see you tomorrow.

Chapter 6

Easy Money

As soon as he thought she would be up, Sal walked next door to Grandma Helene's house. She wasn't related, but she'd been looking after him since he was a child. Over the years, she had baked him cookies, helped him with his homework, and listened to him talk about his dreams.

He knocked on the door and smiled at the sound of Lucky's deep bark. He had bought the Great Dane for Helene when she was threatened by neighborhood bullies. Although he was a cuddle bug, Lucky stood as tall as she did and probably weighed twice as much. The bullying stopped.

Opening the door with a smile, she invited him in. "You're up and about early. Did you eat?"

"No. I have lots to do. I just wanted to tell you what happened yesterday."

"Come. I'll make toast."

Following her past the living room and the gleaming wooden staircase on the right, and the darkened dining room on the left, they entered the heart of the house. Helene's kitchen was bright and spacious, always sparkling clean. Sal knew this house as well as his own. Although next door, it was older and larger, passed down through generations.

Lucky, that gentle giant, sniffed Sal so enthusiastically, he almost knocked him down. *I probably smell like all kinds of interesting plants and animals.* When he sat at the table, the dog rested his chin on the surface and looked up at him with a whine.

"So what's your big news?" Helene put two pieces of bread in the toaster and poured two cups of coffee.

"Well first, a real-life celebrity came to the campground in an RV, and I got lots of pictures."

"That's wonderful." People in town said she never showed any emotion, but Sal could see the interest and pride in her eyes. "Who's this celebrity?"

"Elizabeth Hornwhistle. She's a famous writer."

"Is she pretty?"

"Yeah." He could feel the heat in his cheeks.

"Does Patricia know about this pretty celebrity?"

"No… She's not my girlfriend, you know."

"What's the other big news?"

"Jim and them had a keg party last night and they invited her. Elizabeth. I went out and photographed everything."

Helene knew about Jim. He was one of Salamander's childhood tormentors. "Did you get something good?"

"You're not even going to believe it. Look at these." He passed her a stack of pictures.

Her brow furrowed as she examined them.

"This is my ticket out of town," Sal said.

Helene laid them on the table and looked at him sharply. "You should burn these."

"Hold onto them for me. I'm gonna see what they're worth."

"Please, Salamander, blackmail's dangerous."

He patted her hand and smiled. "It's not blackmail. Just a simple business proposition."

After his visit with Granny Helene, Sal rode his motorbike to the campground. The crisp morning air dispelled any lingering doubts, and the silence, once he parked his bike, filled him with calm. Noiselessly approaching the campsite where the party had been held the night before, he saw Leonard and Freida sitting by the fire.

"Hey, Leonard. Can I talk to you for a sec?"

Looking up from his beer with bruised, droopy eyes, Leonard frowned.

He was a hulking man, with a reputation for brawling, but Sal had bested him before, so he didn't try anything.

"What do you want, Sally?"

"A word. It's private. About last night."

"I'll go get another beer. You two can talk." Freida got up and moved away from the fire.

Sal watched her go. He sat on a log across from Leonard. "What's she doing here with you? Doesn't Mary mind?"

The explosive look on Leonard's face dissipated when he saw the photo Sal handed him.

"That's not what I'm here about, but I'm curious. Frieda has something of a reputation."

"Long story but she didn't have anywhere else to go. Why are you here if not about Mary?"

"It seems like you're running a lucrative business, and I have a proposition for you." He pulled out a couple more pictures and passed them to Leonard. "There are plenty more."

"What do you want?" He sighed.

"I'm in need of funds and thought we could make a deal."

"Do you really want to mess with him?" Leonard asked, referring to the other person in the photo.

"He doesn't need to know. Think of it as a donation."

"How much?"

"Why don't we try ten percent of profits?"

"I don't make as much as you think."

"Would you prefer a flat fee?"

Once they came to an agreement, Sal stood with a smile. Leonard wasn't smiling but the murderous look on his face did nothing to squelch Sal's feeling of triumph. *Next stop, Mrs. Gross. I wonder how much I should ask for.*

He left the campground, heading toward the small neighborhood near the high school where the Grosses lived. The thought of approaching Darla Gross gave Sal vindictive pleasure.

One of his former high school teachers, she had allowed herself to be swayed by popular opinion. Granted, she was only six years older than her students, but she didn't try to stem the bullying. She spoke to him like a stupid child, using his loathed nickname and joining in his classmates' laughter.

She was still beautiful, less flashy than she had been when she began teaching. Her shiny, shoulder-length hair was brown, rather than blonde, and her blouses more modest. At least a decade older, her husband, Coach Gross, was a drinker, and often driven to violent fits of jealousy. Sal heard she was afraid of him and if he was honest, Sal was too. It was hard to defend yourself against that level of crazy. He watched the house from across the street until he was sure she was alone before knocking on the door.

Eyes wide with surprise, a fake smile on her lips, she invited him in and offered him a seat on the couch. "What can I do for you, Sally?"

"It's Sal."

"Oh, yes. I apologize."

He scrutinized the small living room, pristine despite the threadbare furniture, and wondered where their money went. Two full-time high school employees living in a sixty-year-old, eight-hundred-square-foot house and driving fifteen-year-old cars should have plenty. *Savings? Booze?*

Mrs. Gross sat across from him, knees together, hands on her lap, and repeated, "What can I do for you?"

Now came the hard part. No matter how much you dislike someone, or how badly you need money, it was still difficult. Except for Leonard. Leonard should be in jail. Sal shook his head. *Focus.* "I was out taking photos last night," he began, and handed her two. "I have to say I'm a little disappointed."

She studied the pictures, and her shoulders slumped. "He'll kill me if he finds out. Literally. He might kill you too."

"We can avoid that," Sal told her. "I need cash to advance my career.

"We could consider it an informal loan. I might even be able to pay it back some day."

"How much?" she asked. Her voice trembled slightly.

Sal had considered her question before his visit. It couldn't be so much that her husband noticed, and he did have other sources. He scanned the room again. "I don't want to make things difficult for you. What do you do with all your money?"

Her eyebrows rose.

"I'm just curious. You live humbly."

"I'm not sure. John controls our finances. I try to save a little, but I think most of it goes to the bar."

Observing her carefully, Sal wondered if she was telling the truth. "Why don't we try two hundred a month; that's only fifty dollars a week. Will that work?"

She nodded slowly and stood. "Do you need it today?"

He stood as well. "Tomorrow will be fine. I can stop by the fifth wheel." Witnessing her quiet defeat, he felt a tinge of remorse, then he remembered his dream and stiffened his resolve.

Sal's last and most complicated stop that morning was the police station. He understood he had to be careful because even though his father was the chief, police officers tended to take a dim view of extortion.

Chapter 7

Bright New Day

Although Holly had wanted to pack up and leave the night before, she woke to sunshine, chirping birds, and the smoke from nearby campfires. *How could anything bad happen in such a beautiful place?* Raising her face to the sun, she stood absorbing the peace around her. The kitchen window slid open, and the scent of bacon wafted from the RV.

"Ready for breakfast?" Lizzy called.

Holly went inside where Mavis was at her post, concentrating on the cook. Candy was trying to get the little dog's attention, climbing on her back, rolling at her feet, jumping on her tail, but Mavis was impervious. "I smell bacon and… something." She made a face.

"Yeah. Could you open a couple more windows? I was trying to make sunny side up but I had the heat too high. Mavis liked them." Lizzy dished out fried eggs, tater tots, and bacon before handing her a plate.

"This looks a lot better than it smells."

"I might need a little more practice." Carrying her own plate and a bottle of ketchup to the table, Lizzy went back for two cups of coffee before settling across from Holly. "Are you still wanting to leave this morning?"

"It seems so lovely today. Let's take a hike and see if it still feels creepy. Do you think those kids have left?"

"I don't know. We could walk by and check."

"I'll make some sandwiches. We can have a picnic." Holly slipped Mavis a small piece of bacon. "What's that?"

"Hm? The map that guy gave you. This park is huge."

"Can I see?"

"Here." Lizzy passed it to her.

"I marked where our site is and circled the pool and the party site."

"I'm sure we saw more trails than this."

"These are just the roads and main trails, but it'll give us an idea of where we are. Cell phone reception's a little spotty and I don't want to get lost."

By the time they began their hike, the campground was buzzing with departures and arrivals. Tents remained at the combined campsite where the party was held, but they didn't see any sign of life. The fifth wheel, further down, also appeared deserted. The Jeep from the day before was gone. Following the map, Lizzy led Holly deeper into the woods, in the general direction of the lake. Mavis chased butterflies and barked at shadows.

<hr>

Salamander had a busy day. He visited each of his targets and worked a few hours so Brielle could tend her garden. When he finished, he wound his bike through the forest, glancing at Elizabeth's campsite as he passed. She and her friend weren't outside, and the door was closed. *They're probably walking that funny looking little dog.* He weighed his options as he searched for them. *I could sell the pictures and make a name for myself, or I could offer them to her, for a fee. If she really wants to remain hidden, she might pay a lot.* He wondered what a lot might look like. *If I play my hand too soon, I'll be done. No more photos. They might just leave.*

He felt his phone buzz in his pocket and knew Granny Helene was trying to reach him. She was concerned about him, but she didn't understand. He had no choice. "I can take care of myself. You'll see. Just keep those pictures safe," he'd told her.

"You can stay with me for a while. I'd love the company."

"That would just prove Dad right. I have to do this on my own."

Shaking his head to clear it of his last glimpse of her worried face, he focused on his surroundings, searching for two young ladies and their noisy dog. *They should be easy enough to find. Maybe they're even lost and will be glad to see me.* He stayed on the main paths, figuring they wouldn't brave the extensive network of primitive trails.

As he neared the lake, he saw movement ahead, so he pulled over and camouflaged his bike in the bushes. Creeping forward with his camera, he began shooting indiscriminately. The birds went quiet and a snapped twig broke the silence. He slowly lowered his camera and caught movement out of the corner of his eye. The world went black.

Rather than leading directly to the lake, the road Lizzy chose curved in the opposite direction and wound through the woods, crisscrossed by numerous rough trails. After two hours, sweating and covered in tiny scratches and bug bites, Lizzy suggested they rest. "I need water."

"Me too. There's a log we can sit on."

They sat and retrieved their water bottles from their backpacks.

"Should we eat something while we're at it?" Holly asked.

Mavis barked and Lizzy's stomach growled.

"Two of a kind." She giggled and handed Lizzy a club sandwich. Mavis watched her carefully as she unwrapped her own. She laid the sandwich on the log and pulled out three bowls, one for water and two for food, setting them at her feet.

Mavis had other ideas. While Holly was pouring water, she jumped up with her front paws on the log and snatched the sandwich, running as far as she could before her leash pulled her up short.

"Hey," Holly shouted. "You get back here with that."

"Do you want half of mine?"

"I brought five, but still." She poured some kitty kibble in a bowl for Candy and watched Mavis inhale her sandwich.

"We can split the extra one," Lizzy said, unwrapping her second.

"You probably shouldn't eat too much at once. We still have a long hike back."

"I know, but I'm so hungry." A blur of red and white accompanied the crunch of footsteps. She placed her hand on Holly's arm. "Shh. There's someone over there," she whispered. She squinted at the tall, thin figure skulking through the trees. "I think it's Jim." The fine hair on her arms stood on end.

"Did he see us?" Holly whispered back.

"I don't know, but he's headed back the way we came. What's he doing out here?"

"Is that a rhetorical question?"

Lizzy's eyebrows rose. "I guess you can't answer it. Unless you know him a lot better than I do." She chuckled. Her eyes followed him until he disappeared, then she took another bite of her sandwich.

Mavis slunk toward the log, focused on Candy's snack, but Holly held her back with a foot. "No you don't, you little thief."

"Oh, look," Lizzy said, pointing.

Holly aimed her phone and tried to get a picture, but the white-tailed deer seemed to sense their presence and quickly vanished. "Aww. She was gorgeous."

"If we pay attention we might see another one. I've seen some little critters too. One was a possum I think."

Two delicious club sandwiches and a bottle of water later, Lizzy patted her stomach and groaned. "I don't know if I can walk now."

"I'm not going to say I told you so, but—"

"You just did."

"Oh. Yeah. I told you not to eat both of them. We still have a two-hour walk back."

"At least it's not uphill. Ready?"

"Curl into a ball and I'll roll you." Holly giggled.

"Very funny." Lizzy stood and brushed the crumbs off her jeans, sending Mavis into an energetic bout of sniffing and digging. "I think Mavis just ate a bug."

"I wouldn't doubt it. Silly puppy."

Old-growth trees filtered the sunlight, and a light gust of wind gave Lizzy goosebumps. "We should head back. I'm getting cold."

"You are definitely not a native South Dakotan yet. This feels like summer."

"Summer is over ninety degrees. Not seventy."

"Potayto potahto." Holly stood and moved toward the path. "If we go a little farther we'll reach the lake. Let's take a look at least."

"Mavis wants to go that way too."

"We shall heed her divine Highness by all means."

Lizzy snorted. She couldn't tell how far they had walked when the barking began. Mavis yanked against her leash. She dashed forward with a great leap into the air, then regrouped when the harness stopped her momentum and repeated the process. Surprisingly strong, she made it difficult to hold on. Lizzy could glimpse the lake between the trees. "What is it Mavis? Can you smell the water?"

"Good thing she's got her harness on," Holly said.

When they were almost to the clearing, the dog changed her course, cutting in front of Holly and pulling Lizzy into the bushes. "Let's follow her. It's probably just a rabbit or something, but she's in stubborn mode."

Holly picked up Candy and followed them through the undergrowth.

After the second time she tripped, Lizzy was tempted to unclip the leash. "Nutty dog," she muttered.

As they drew near the water, Mavis' barking grew louder and more insistent. She passed through the tree line then stopped abruptly. Standing stiff-legged at the edge of the clearing, she howled.

The first to see the body, Lizzy tossed the end of the leash to Holly and took out her phone. Taking pictures as she advanced, she documented the scene before touching anything.

He was face down in shallow water. Heart beating so hard her chest hurt, Lizzy approached him cautiously, then bent over and tried to turn him. He didn't budge. She crouched and using both hands, pushed his left shoulder and hip. The body bobbed slightly to the right. Frustrated, Lizzy stood over him, straddling his body. She pulled his left side and pushed on the right, finally managing to flip him onto his back. Although he was obviously dead, she checked for his pulse and called 911, then took more pictures of the scene.

Mavis sat quietly, her work apparently done. Face expressionless, Holly sat in the sand next to the little dog.

"Do you recognize him?" Lizzy asked.

"He works here."

She nodded.

"Why do you keep finding bodies?"

"Just lucky I guess."

Holly glanced at her sharply, then sagged when she saw her face. "I'm sorry."

"Technically, Mavis has found the last two." She sat next to them to wait.

Chapter 8

Don't Leave Town

Lizzy's eyes closed briefly as she sat absorbing the warm afternoon sunshine. The quiet lapping of the lake water and the smell of fish, soil, and some kind of flowers, lulled her into a peaceful state. She felt Mavis shift next to her and heard the shrill sound of sirens in the distance.

Chaos rapidly erased any semblance of tranquility. Barking, sirens, and the noisy entrance of investigators transformed the clearing into a busy crime scene. Corporal Quirk, following a portly man in a suit, scowled at Lizzy and Holly. "You again?"

The man in the suit caught sight of the victim and completely lost control of himself. The medical examiner commanded the other officers to restrain him before he could destroy any evidence. Officer Garcia and a third officer took his arms as he shouted obscenities. He insisted they release him, kicking and twisting in their grasps.

"Chief," Garcia said urgently, "You have to let him do his job so we can catch whoever did this."

Lizzy glanced at Holly but kept her lips firmly sealed. Mavis whined softly.

The medical examiner approached the victim and Corporal Quirk began taking photographs. Squinting at him, she thought something was off. He tripped several times and dropped the camera.

"Has someone moved the body?" the ME demanded.

"Yes, sir." Lizzy said, standing. "I photographed everything first, but I wanted to make sure I couldn't save him."

"Show me how you found him."

She tried to ignore his intimidating glare as she pulled up the photo with shaky hands and offered him her phone.

"I *am* sorry, but I couldn't just leave him there without checking."

He studied the photo and swiped through the gallery. "Well done, young lady." His tone softened marginally. "I appreciate your attention to detail." He returned her phone and provided her with a business card. "Send me those, please."

Lizzy assured him she would and looked through the gallery again as he returned to the body. She noticed details she had missed, like the unusual tread on the single footprint in the wet sand. She couldn't catch the medical examiner's words as he spoke quietly into a recorder. When Quirk approached him, however, his high-pitched voice echoed across the clearing, vying with Mavis. The ME told him the cause of death was likely drowning despite a severe head wound. The time of death was recent. "I can be more exact once I get him on the table. Let's transport him to the hospital as soon as possible."

Garcia startled Lizzy when he appeared at her side and bent his head to look over her shoulder. Absorbed in the crime scene, she hadn't yet sent her email.

"What are you doing with those?" he demanded.

"The medical examiner asked me to send them."

His shoulders relaxed. "I'll need to collect some basic information from you, then I'll stop by for a formal statement later. Please don't leave town."

"What do you need?"

"Name, permanent address, destination, and names and contact information of two people who know you." He proffered a clipboard and a pen.

Lizzy wrote down her information and passed the board to Holly.

"Are family members okay?" she asked.

"One of them can be a family member."

When finished, she handed the clipboard back and he scanned the results.

"Captain Jason Schneider of the Harperstown police department?" he asked Lizzy.

"Yes. He knows me well."

"Holly *Schneider?*"

"He's my brother."

"Thank you. You can return to your campsite now. I'll be by later."

He strode off to confer with Quirk.

Lizzy helped Holly up and said, "Ready, Mavis? It'll be dinner time soon."

"Only you could think about eating at a time like this."

Mavis barked twice and wagged her tail.

"See? It's not just me. Although I'll need to wash my hands."

"I have some hand sanitizer."

"I think it's going to take more than that." Lizzy shuddered.

<hr>

By the time they reached the motor home, Lizzy was obsessing over her hands. She washed them twice and then showered, finishing with hand sanitizer.

Holly didn't speak. She watched as Lizzy washed her hands again and applied more sanitizer. Then she said, "Come sit down and have some coffee."

Lizzy sat across from Holly and lifted her cup. She looked at it and set it back down.

"Do you want to talk about it?"

"No, not really."

"I've seen you like this before. You act all no-nonsense, but it gnaws at you. You need to let it out."

She pressed her lips together and shook her head.

"What you did was very brave."

"It wasn't brave. I had to do it. What if he was still alive and I left him there?"

Holly could see the rise and fall of her chest. "Do you need a paper bag?"

"No, I'm okay. I *will* be okay. I wish Jason was here."

"I think that's the first time I've ever heard you bring him up."

"He makes me feel safe," Lizzy mumbled.

"We could call him."

Lizzy shook her head again. "I don't want him to know."

Contemplating her friend, Holly wondered why. She didn't understand, but she didn't need to. *They'll figure it out.* "Do you want pizza?"

"Frozen pizza or real pizza?"

"Real pizza."

"Will it take long?"

"Half an hour. You feed Mavis and it'll be ready before you know it."

Lizzy's stomach growled.

⚬⚬⚬

Grateful to Holly for pulling her out of her dark thoughts, Lizzy was able to concentrate on the case at hand. The chief's response at the crime scene was highly unusual. She wanted to discuss it, but Holly was sensitive. *I'll wait until she's had time to process. Almost guaranteed finding the body was more traumatic for her, even though she's trying to help me deal with it.*

Scents of cheese and fresh herbs wafted through the RV as Holly removed her creation from the oven. Lizzy breathed in and sighed. "That smells so good. I might be drooling a little."

"Just a little?" Holly giggled.

Mavis, too busy projecting her ESP on Holly to move, barked and glanced briefly at the door. Someone knocked and Lizzy moaned. "Noo. I don't want to share. Tell him to go away."

Holly snickered and opened the door for Officer Garcia. "Come in. We were just about to have supper."

"Don't let it get cold. We can talk while you eat."

"Oh, good. Lizzy can be dangerous when she's *hangry*."

"I would take offense, but there might be a grain of truth there." Lizzy smiled. "Have a seat, Officer. Would you like a slice?"

He gazed longingly at the pizza. "Where did you get that? We don't have any decent pizza places in town."

"Holly made it."

"I wouldn't say no to a small slice, if you don't mind sharing."

"I can always make another." Holly cut the pizza into slices and set the tray and three plates on the table. "Would you like something to drink?"

"Whatever you're having is fine."

"Coffee?"

"Sure."

"Where's your sidekick?"

"Quirk?" His eyebrows rose.

Lizzy grinned.

"We're having some issues at the station." He accepted a cup of coffee from Holly. "I checked up on you two before I came over and was assured that you could be trusted and possibly of assistance." He bit into the pizza and groaned.

Holly smiled.

"A man after my own heart," Lizzy said.

He finished chewing and said, "The victim was the chief's son. The chief is currently hospitalized and under sedation. Corporal Quirk is…"

"Unhelpful?" Lizzy asked.

After a pause, Garcia said, "Your words, not mine. Let's just say that if he's leading the investigation, you probably won't make it to your conference."

"Oh, no. I hadn't thought of that. Has anyone spoken to the campground managers? Will they let us stay here?"

"We've informed them your stay will be extended."

Lizzy selected her third slice of pizza. "How can we help?"

"We'll start with your statements and then maybe I can just bounce ideas off you as we investigate? This is my first homicide, but Captain Schneider tells me you've helped him in the past."

Lizzy opened her mouth, then shut it again. She was going to tell him it was Mavis but then remembered Jason telling her not to mention that to his chief. Perhaps he had a point. She didn't know how much the little dog really understood, but she always seemed to lead her in the right direction.

Chapter 9

Fallout

After Salamander had left that morning, Helene sat in her living room, staring out the front window. *I should have told him more. He's poking a hornet's nest. How can I warn him when I don't know who's behind it?*

Lucky sensed her unease and whined. She stroked his head and waited.

Unsure of what she was waiting for, she knew it when it arrived in the form of her grandson. "Come in," she called when he knocked.

"Hi Gran."

"Marty."

He sat next to her on the sofa and took her hand. "I know how much you loved Sally…"

Helene pulled her hand away. "Is he dead?" she asked woodenly.

"How did you know?"

"A premonition, I suppose. What happened?"

"He drowned."

"You think it was an accident?"

"Why? Do you know something?"

Helene went back to staring out the window.

"I just want you to know I'm sorry and if you need anything at all, I'm here for you."

She felt an inappropriate laugh well up inside. Blood or not, Marty had never lifted a finger to help her with anything.

"Gran?"

He was annoying her. "Leave me now. I need to be by myself."

"I'm sorry Gran," he mumbled, then turned and shuffled toward the door.

She didn't move, but after he left, a single tear rolled down her cheek. *My sweet boy. What will I ever do without you? Why didn't you listen?*

━━━━━━ ⁘⟨⟩⁘ ━━━━━━

After the pizza was gone and they had finished giving their statements, Officer Garcia handed them each a business card bearing his telephone number and thanked them. Holly saw him out while Lizzy began the cleanup.

At the door, she asked, "Is it safe to have a campfire at night? Have those guys who tried to break in left the campground?"

"You should be fine now. They've been warned and they've all checked out."

"You know them?"

"Yes. A petty thief and a couple of kids from the high school football team. Jim was arrested and I notified the coach. He'll see to it that it doesn't happen again."

"Are you up for a campfire then?" Lizzy asked when he was gone.

"We could make s'mores."

"Mm." Lizzy's phone rang. "Be right back," she said, and went outside to answer.

"Hi Jason," she said into the phone.

"I hear you're back in the thick of things," he said.

She could hear the smile in his voice and wished again that he was there with her. "It was Mavis."

"How did I know you'd say that?" He chuckled. "What do you think of Officer Garcia?"

"So far, I'm thinking we should convince him to take the open position in Harperstown."

The momentary silence was oppressive. "Why is that?"

"He reminds me of Barker. Not his appearance, but the way he performs his duties.

"He would fit in well with your team and he's young, so there's a lot of potential."

"We'll see if you feel the same way by the time you solve the case."

"Me?" Lizzy laughed. "Maybe Mavis."

"Do you need anything? Is there anything I can do?"

"This has helped. I realized this afternoon that you've always been there in a crisis and…" She was leery of saying too much. "I missed you."

"I wish I could be there for you, and I want you to know, if things get worse and you need me to, I'll fly down there and do what I can to help. Just let me know."

"Thank you. That means a lot." She was relieved he couldn't see her because her traitorous eyes were leaking. "I have to go, but I'll keep you updated."

"Okay. Say hi to Holly and be careful."

"I will."

Lizzy disconnected and took a stroll to get her emotions in check. She didn't want Holly to notice her emotional state and try to meddle. Her feet led her past the party campsite where only a single tent stood in the waning light.

Turning to make an about face, she glanced down to find Mavis at her feet. "What are you doing here?"

Mavis barked once.

"Well, let's head back now. It's getting dark."

They walked back together, Mavis happily stopping to sniff everything in her path without restraint.

As soon as they reached the campsite entrance, Holly ran toward them, clutching Candy to her chest. "Thank goodness. Mavis disappeared and I couldn't find her. I was beside myself."

"I turned around and there she was. I imagine she was in her pen. How did she get out?"

"She burrowed right under it. We'll have to keep an eye on her."

Lizzy picked Mavis up and hugged her. "I'm glad you're okay, puppy."

"I see you've got the fire going. Ready to toast some marshmallows?"

"I'm sorry about Mavis. Thanks for not being mad."

"We both know how wily she is. How could I be mad?"

<hr>

Lucky was a patient dog, but eventually he got hungry enough that he gave Helene a nudge. When she ignored him, he walked into the kitchen and returned with his bowl, setting it on her lap. He sat in front of her and barked once.

"Oh dear." Helene snapped to attention. "I'd better get my head outta the clouds." She fed her dog and took him for a walk, not bothering with a leash because if he wasn't going to behave, she couldn't stop him. *A saddle would be more effective.* She chuckled and placed her hand on his back. "You're all I've got now, boy."

When she and Lucky returned from their walk, Helene closed the curtains and sat at the glass coffee table with Sal's photos. Spreading them out in front of her, she studied them one at a time and placed them in two piles. She was grieving, but she was also filled with rage. Family or not, whoever killed Salamander would pay.

She didn't sleep that night. She lay in bed and stared at the ceiling. Dawn found her in the kitchen, making lemon bars with powdered sugar on top. When they were cool, she carried them next door and rang the front bell.

Sal's mother, Marjorie, answered the door in an old housecoat, hard plastic rollers in her bleached hair. Deep purple shadows sat below her red-rimmed eyes.

"I brought Sal's favorite cookies and my condolences."

Marjorie eyed the cookies as if they might bite and took a step back.

"Is there anything I can do to help with the funeral?"

"Stay away from me. This is all your fault."

"Oh? How do you figure?"

"You… you spoiled him. You encouraged his wild ideas. If it wasn't for you he'd be safe, off at college somewhere."

"And you made him stubborn. If you hadn't pushed so hard…" Helene stopped. "This is ridiculous. He's gone and we'll both miss him."

She turned to leave, waiting for the door to slam.

"Wait. I'm sorry. Can I have the cookies?"

Helene turned slowly and handed her the plate.

"My husband's in the hospital. They had to sedate him when he saw Salamander and now they suspect him of murder." Her entire body shook.

Not a demonstrative woman, Helene nevertheless put her arm around Marjorie and led her back inside. "Let me make you some tea," she said.

Chapter 10

Helene Investigates

Sitting in front of the campfire the next morning, Lizzy took a sip of coffee and watched a bright pink bicycle approach. As it got closer, she could see a tiny elderly woman pedaling vigorously. Her white hair was cemented in place, impervious to the gentle breeze, her arms and legs impossibly thin.

The woman rode right up to Lizzy and dismounted. "Good morning." She seemed congenial, although she didn't smile, her fathomless black eyes looking straight into Lizzy's.

"Good morning." Lizzy rose and then wished she hadn't. She towered over the woman, who was no more than four foot five, possibly eighty pounds. "How can I help you?"

"I'm looking for Elizabeth Hornwhistle."

"That would be me."

The woman's face creased into a thousand folds when she chuckled mirthlessly. "The poor boy got it all wrong," she said. "Could we go inside and talk?"

Lizzy nodded and led the way, calling, "Holly. Company," as she opened the door. She indicated a bench at the fold-down table and asked her guest if she'd like some coffee or tea.

"Coffee please."

When Holly appeared with Candy, the woman held out her hands for the kitten. "How sweet," she said.

Lizzy ferried refreshments to the table and sat next to Holly. Mavis was being suspiciously quiet, sitting at the woman's feet and gazing up at her.

"Do you have dog treats in your pockets?"

"No, they just love me for some reason." She reached down and stroked Mavis' ears.

"I'm Helene, by the way. I hear you found poor Salamander yesterday."

Lizzy canted her head. "Salamander?"

"The murder victim."

"How did you hear about that?"

"My grandson stopped by. He knew we were close."

"Did he also tell you where we were staying?"

"No, that was Salamander. Did you meet him?"

"I met him when we checked in," Holly said. "I didn't know his name, but he seemed very polite."

"He went by Sal these days. The other kids bullied him and called him Sally." Helene stared into the distance for a moment. "He spent a lot of time at my house, even as a child. I think I might have been his only friend." She blinked rapidly. "Yesterday morning he left something with me that might help find his killer. I can't give it to his pa; you'll see why. And I can't give it to my grandson because he's not all that bright."

"Who's your grandson?" Lizzy asked.

"His name's Marty Quirk. He's a policeman."

"We've met."

Helene nodded.

"Why come to us?"

She pulled an envelope from the jacket of her vibrant aqua-colored velour tracksuit and opened it. "He took these day before yesterday. I've sorted them into categories, the first being you two." She handed a stack to Lizzy. "He told me all about the beautiful celebrity author staying here and how his luck was going to change. He didn't tell you about them?"

Flipping through the photographs, Lizzy shook her head before rising and walking into the bedroom. When she returned, she handed a hardcover book to Helene. "Look at the picture on the back. *Really* look at it."

Helene did so; then she scrutinized the two friends, her eyes glittering.

"I can see how he got mixed up. Are you relations?"

"No. Can we keep these?" Lizzy smiled and passed them to Holly.

"I don't see why not. You're not really suspects since you didn't even know him."

"These other ones though—Salamander was trying to get snapshots of you at the party, but when he developed his film, he found what he called an accidental goldmine. I warned him black-mail's dangerous, but he said it wasn't blackmail. It was his way to get out of his parents' house and make a name for himself."

Lizzy pressed her lips together and held out her hand.

"You won't understand them unless I explain." Helene gave Lizzy the second stack. As they went through the photos, Helene described evidence of drugs, infidelity, and insurance fraud. "This is his pa, the chief of police, and that's not his wife."

"Would Salamander have confronted him?"

"Doubtful, but the woman might've told him."

"Could the motive have been something completely unrelated? I mean, could it have been an argument over a girl, or money?"

"He kept his head down. He was bullied and teased. He didn't have a girlfriend, and he spent all his money on cameras. And there's the timing. Mark my words; one of those people killed him."

"Can we share these with Officer Garcia?"

"Do what you think best. I just wanted to keep them from Marty and the chief. I don't know you, but since you're part of it, I thought... well, I guess I thought you could at least be witness to them."

"That makes sense."

They wrapped up their conversation and Helene said goodbye, thanking them for their help. Mavis followed her out the door, belatedly barking and wagging her tail. "You're a weird dog," Lizzy said, as she watched the tiny old woman mount her bicycle and pedal back toward the exit.

"How old do you think she is?" Holly asked from the doorway.

"At least ninety."

"She's going to miss him."

Racing into the RV to dig out her notebook, Lizzy sat at the desk in her room and wrote down everything she could remember about Helene. She was winding down when Holly tapped on the door and stuck her head inside.

"You okay?"

"Wonderful. Isn't she a fascinating character?"

"I suppose she is." Holly smiled. "Let's go swimming. I made sandwiches."

"Sounds good. I need to call Kirk and let him know what happened. We should look back through the photos of the crime scene too and decide what to do with the ones Helene gave us."

"I know, but right now we need a break."

"Agreed. Let me just make a quick call so I don't forget."

Kirk answered on the first ring. She owed her new life in South Dakota to him, and she was relying on his help to stay incognito in Los Angeles.

"Lizzy! Getting close?"

She paused momentarily. "No, we're still in Serenity. We were supposed to check out tomorrow, but we've been delayed."

"You're still going to make it, aren't you?"

"I hope so. There's been a murder and we've been told not to leave town."

The line went silent.

"Kirk? That doesn't mean I won't be there."

"There's no telling how long it will take them to solve the case— I didn't want to tell you this, but I wasn't sure if you were ready to come out of hiding, so I have a backup."

"You think I'm making it up?"

"No, of course not. But it's so soon. I thought you might have a change of heart."

"Well, don't count me out yet, okay? Hopefully, we'll get out of here in time."

"I hope you can, but I'd like to see you, even if you can't make it to the conference. I've missed you."

With plenty of time to think as she peddled toward town, Helene decided to visit the two people she thought the police would overlook. Salamander had probably disregarded them as well, but she wanted to be sure.

Her first stop was the mayor's office. When she stepped off the elevator, his new receptionist glanced up from filing her nails and said, "Do you have an appointment?" in a bored voice.

"Just let him know Helene is here to see him."

"He doesn't see anyone without an appointment."

Helene preferred not to argue. She walked right past the receptionist and entered the mayor's office without knocking. It always reminded Helene of a library. His mahogany desk sat in the center, large enough to serve as a dining table and floor to ceiling bookshelves lined the walls. Leatherbound books and binders spilled from the shelves. The mayor put a hand over the telephone receiver and motioned her to have a seat. Waving the panicked receptionist away, he finished his call.

"I have an appointment, Bart. Let me put you through to my secretary and she can schedule lunch later this week."

He disconnected and grinned with large unnaturally white teeth. "To what do I owe this pleasure?"

"I want to ask you about something personal. I don't mean you any harm. I just need to know."

His brows furrowed slightly. "Go ahead."

"I'm sure you've heard about Salamander's murder." She paused.

"Yes. I'm so sorry. I know how close you were."

"I think he got himself into trouble over some photos he took. He was trying to get snapshots of a celebrity and got much more than he bargained for." Helene handed the mayor the one of his niece Brielle tending her marijuana plants.

"The police already have them, and I imagine they won't pay this one any mind, but I wanted you to know so you can put a stop to it."

He studied the picture. "Foolish girl."

"You didn't know anything about this?"

"Of course not. I'll see to it that she stops."

Helene nodded. "Salamander really liked Brielle and Emiliano, so I doubt they would've been on his list of *business propositions*, but I just wanted to check in with you."

He paused, with an increased furrowing of his brows at her terminology. "I appreciate the heads up. Let me know if there's anything I can do for you."

"Thank you, Mayor. How's the baby?"

"He came early and there were some complications, so they're still at the hospital. The campground is temporarily closed, and Emiliano is staying here in town with Brielle's mama."

"You know there are still guests at the campground, right?"

"Yes. They'll be there until the police wrap up their investigation. I suppose it's good timing."

"Yes, I suppose it is. I won't take up any more of your time." She stood. "Thank you for seeing me."

"You're welcome. Stop by any time."

She said goodbye and left his office. As she passed the vacant reception desk on her way to the elevator, she couldn't help wondering how long the new receptionist would last.

Her second, less pleasant visit was with Mr. Gross, the local football coach. Although he had turned the team around and wielded considerable power within the community, he was almost universally disliked. His harsh bombastic personality cowed players and parents alike.

Helene parked her bicycle outside the sports complex where his office was located and knocked before entering.

Once inside, she observed his red-faced countenance behind a scarred wooden desk. She served on the school board but had never spoken to the coach individually; she had never felt the need. That day, however, she had a compelling reason and hoped he wouldn't make a scene.

"Good afternoon. How can I help you?" he asked.

She decided to try the same tactic she used with the mayor. Beginning with the same wording about Sal's murder and not meaning him any harm, she showed him a snapshot. "I'm sure you were just busting your players and sending them home, but Salamander was talking nonsense about taking donations from certain people and I wanted to know if he talked to you about his little *hobby*." Helene wrinkled her nose with distaste, hoping to demonstrate her sympathy.

The coach's face turned a deeper shade of red and the hand that held the photo shook almost imperceptibly. "What do you want?" he asked quietly.

"Nothing. Just information. Salamander spoke to a lot of people and got himself into trouble. I just want to know who he talked to so I can figure out what he was saying and who he might've made mad."

His shoulders and his grip on the photo relaxed. "I would have been angry if he accused me of something, but he didn't get around to me."

Helene nodded. "Do you know of anyone else he might have talked to?"

"No. Sorry. Can I keep this picture?"

"Of course." She smiled. "Thanks for your help." She left his office and got back on her bike. *I don't trust him. Maybe Art can vouch for his whereabouts.* She rode toward the *Trough* on Main Street.

A strict teetotaler, Helene rarely stepped foot into the *Trough*, but she knew Art, the proprietor well.

He was married to her late sister-in-law's great niece and was often present at family gatherings.

When she entered, Art stood polishing the glassware behind the bar in the quiet of the early afternoon and squinted into the bright light flooding through the open door. "Auntie Helene? Is that you?"

"It sure is. How's my favorite nephew?"

He grinned. "Can I get you some iced tea?"

"No, I'm fine." She scanned the empty bar and lowered her voice as she approached. "I really just wanted to ask you if you remember what time the coach was in here yesterday."

Art's eyebrows shot up. "Coach? He was here all afternoon."

"That's all I wanted to know."

"Is this about Sal?" He put his elbows on the bar.

"Yes. Just checking a few things."

"I'm very sorry, Auntie. I know you'll miss him."

"I will. Thanks for your help." She turned and left the bar before he could ask more questions. She didn't want to talk about her feelings; she just wanted to find out who killed her boy.

She mounted her bicycle and pedaled two blocks down Main Street to the Masterpiece Salon. Serenity was a typical little town. Sprawling, like many towns in Texas, it gave the impression that it was larger than it actually was. Travelers and weekenders plumped up the economy, but the locals knew where to go for the best prices and reliable gossip.

Conversation stopped and heads swiveled when the bell jangled and Helene stepped inside. Wanda, wearing her signature tie-dyed smock, rushed to greet her and the chatter resumed as if there had been no interruption.

"Helene. I wondered if you would come today. I'm so sorry about Sal," Wanda said, and was joined by the others in her condolences. *Such a terrible thing… Who could do such a thing?... I heard it was some traveling book writer… We should close down that campground; too many strangers passing through.*

When Helene didn't comment, she once again became the object of scrutiny. They all waited for her to weigh in on the discussion. Mentally rolling her eyes, she said, "I don't know who did it but I'm sure my Marty will find out."

"Well let's get you beautified for the funeral," Wanda said firmly. "That'll be one less thing for you to worry about."

The other women in the salon paid no heed to Wanda's warning glare and continued gossiping quietly among themselves. Tuning them out, Helene focused on her hairdresser's ongoing stream of chatter and the feel of warm water and gentle fingers in her hair.

Chapter 11

The Muddy Boot

Holly marveled at how quickly Lizzy browned in the sun. Granted, the high SPF sunscreen Holly used blocked out some of the rays, but without it she would look like a radish. She stretched out on a pool-side recliner, partially shaded by an umbrella, and watched Lizzy playing in the water with Mavis.

"She's swimming circles around you."

"Literally." She swam to the side and held on, kicking her feet. "Is it lunch time yet?"

"It can be."

"Come on, Mavis, let's get a snack."

Mavis followed her to the stairs and hopped out of the pool, stopping to shake vigorously. She rolled on her back, wiggling on the hot cement, then trotted to the recliner and sat at Holly's feet. Lizzy sat on an adjacent chair, but she didn't have food, so the little dog ignored her.

"I made Mavis her own special sandwich," Holly said. "Scrambled eggs and veggies." She placed the quarter sandwich in a bowl and set it on the ground before handing Lizzy hers.

"Tuna salad today." Holly took a bite of her sandwich. "We should have brought Candy. I felt bad leaving her alone."

"It's hard to know what's best. She's still so little. How long have we been here?"

"A couple of hours."

"Let's have another dip and we can head back."

"Okay. Is the water cold?"

"It's a little chilly but you'll warm up when you move around. The absolute worst is when it's sweltering outside, and the pool feels like a warm bath."

The water was refreshing, and Lizzy was right. She warmed up as she raced Mavis back and forth across the pool. By the time she got out, the sun felt hot, and she was tempted to go back in. She thought of Candy though, and decided it was time to return to the RV.

"Ready to go?"

"I love the water so much; I could stay all day. But yes, I suppose it's time." Lizzy towel-dried Mavis and put her harness on her, then slung her own towel around her shoulders and grabbed her backpack. "Let's stop by that dumpster."

Holly hadn't noticed the dumpster. It was sitting in a narrow gravel path outside the fence, behind an adjacent building that she thought might house showers and changing rooms.

Tossing their garbage into the dumpster, Lizzy stilled and canted her head. "Call Garcia and ask him to meet us here."

Holly dialed his number and as she waited for him to answer, Mavis began to bark. A slight man with heavy dark brows strolled around the corner of the building, pausing momentarily when he saw Lizzy, then racing toward her. He spoke rapidly in Spanish, waving his arms, causing Mavis' barking to intensify as she strained against her leash.

"Officer Garcia," he answered.

"This is Holly Schneider." She grasped her phone tightly and backed away from the dumpster. "Could you meet us at the campground pool? Quickly?"

"Are you safe? What's all that noise?"

"I think we're safe but please hurry."

She disconnected but remained where she was, not wanting to escalate the situation.

Surprised by the heavily pregnant brunette who rounded the corner next, Holly gasped. She was one of the suspects in the photos Helene had given them. She approached the man and lay her callused hand on his forearm.

She called him Emiliano and spoke to him in quiet Spanish. He calmed as she spoke, then turning and addressing Lizzy, she said, "I'm sorry if my husband startled you. What are you doing back here?"

"We were swimming and decided to throw our lunch bags away before we returned to our camp site."

"You're the guests at site forty-eight, right? Pool season isn't until May."

"I'm sorry. The weather is lovely, and I didn't see any signs."

"We haven't been able to check the chemical levels, so it isn't safe. You didn't take the dog in did you?"

"She loves to swim and again, we didn't see any signs."

The woman sighed, glancing past Lizzy when Garcia pulled up in his cruiser. "You called the cops?"

"Before you came. It's unrelated."

Strolling over to Holly, Lizzy handed her the leash. "I need to speak with Garcia. Make sure they don't take anything from the dumpster."

<hr>

Officer Garcia got out of his cruiser and waited for Lizzy to approach with a quizzical look on his face. She opened her phone as she walked, handing it to him when she stopped by his side. "See those footprints in the mud?"

He enlarged the picture on her screen. "Yeah?"

"There's a muddy boot in that dumpster with the same tread."

Suddenly alert, Garcia pulled on a pair of disposable gloves and strode to the dumpster. He scanned the contents and grabbed the boot. "Do you recognize this boot, Brielle?"

"Yes. It went missing a couple of days ago. Why's it so muddy?"

"Es tuyo, ¿verdad?" she asked her husband.

"Creo que sí." He nodded.

"What's this all about?"

Garcia placed the boot on the ground and rooted through the garbage, emerging with the second one. "I'll have to take these for the time being. Would you like a receipt?"

Brielle's voice rose. "Why? What's going on?"

"Calm down. They look like a match for some footprints we found down near the lake. It might be nothing."

Eyes round, she stiffened, then grabbed her belly and doubled over. "The baby. It's coming. Take me to the hospital."

"Do you have a bag packed?"

She shot rapid-fire instructions to her husband, who sprinted around the corner of the building.

Garcia helped her get settled in the back seat and placed the boots in his trunk. Emiliano ran toward the cruiser with an overnight bag and joined his wife.

"I'll be back to talk to you after I get them to the hospital," Garcia said. He slid into the driver's seat and backed the cruiser down the narrow road with his siren blaring.

Lizzy and Holly watched them go. Mavis' sudden silence was deafening. She wagged her tail.

"What was that?" Holly asked.

Lizzy showed her the photo she had shown Garcia. "The boots don't prove he's the killer," she said. "Just that someone wearing those boots was at the crime scene."

"He didn't look happy when he saw you by the dumpster."

"No, he seemed angry. Now I'm hot and wish we could get back in the pool."

"We probably could but…"

"I know. Garcia will be stopping by, and we need showers."

"And Candy's waiting." Holly smiled.

Holly's showers always took longer than Lizzy's because her hair was so long. Lizzy wandered outside while she waited. She had gradually discovered dozens of extras built into the RV, like the outdoor awning that could be raised and lowered with the push of a button, and Bluetooth speakers. She didn't think the awning was necessary, but by opening the compartment, they had access to a gas grill and a counter where they could cook outdoors. She connected the playlist on her phone to the speakers and sat in one of the camp chairs.

If I had known about this kind of house on wheels, I could have moved around. It has everything I need. Would I have liked that? She thought she probably would have. *But then I wouldn't have met Holly. Or Jason. Or Mavis. I did the right thing.* She closed her eyes and conjured her main character. Rachel had an adventurous life, often finding herself in dangerous situations and having to rely on her finely honed problem-solving skills to escape. *Maybe she can live in an RV while she's undercover.* Lizzy still hadn't figured out what kind of religious-themed crime would require a high-level spy like Rachel to become involved. *She could be on vacation. Or the church in question could be a front for an international—augh. A catholic church would be so much easier; the Pope, nuns' habits, ancient cathedrals...am I really married to this idea?*

Holly opened the door and saved her from her tangled thoughts. "What are you listening to?"

"It's a mishmash. Let's cook outside tonight. It's so warm."

"How about something light? Steaks and salad?"

"That sounds great. Do you know how to use the grill?"

Holly wandered over to the grill she was pointing at and inspected it. She found the attachment for the propane and hooked it up, before turning it on. Rewarded with a flame, she said, "It's good to go. Can you grill the steaks?"

Lizzy paused before she answered. "How picky are you?"

"I like mine well done. That means cook it until it's not pink in the middle, even if you burn it a little."

"I like mine pink. Do I just leave yours on longer?"

Holly giggled. "You should make the salad."

"I can do that. I think."

Lizzy had watched Holly make salad and she had eaten it, of course, but when she surveyed her finished product, she wasn't too impressed. She put the bowl on the table as Holly entered with a plate of steaming steaks. "Those smell so good."

"Mavis thinks so too."

The little dog whined and groaned dramatically.

"Cut it out. You know you'll get some." Lizzy set the table, and ferried salad dressing, steak sauce, and two beers from the refrigerator before sitting across from Holly.

"A very interesting-looking salad." Holly speared a long piece of red bell pepper.

"Yeah. Sorry. I wasn't thinking about the overall picture when I was chopping."

Holly grinned. "It's still salad and it tastes great. I hope I cooked your steak how you like it."

"It's perfect."

"When do you suppose Officer Garcia will get here?"

"I don't know but we should probably decide what to do about those photos before he comes."

"What do you mean?"

"Well, some of them, like the drug dealer—those are obvious. We should give them to the police, right? But what about some of the others, like Brielle tending her pot plants? It's illegal but do we really want to involve the police? Helene said it could cause her a lot of problems."

"Is it our place to decide what the police should know? Any of them could be suspects."

"Are we going to share the pictures of us too?" Lizzy handed Mavis a piece of gristle and almost lost a finger. "I guess the real question is: do we trust Garcia? What will he do with them? Will he

"Remember how mad Jason got? I think we'd better just hand them over and cross our fingers."

Slightly annoyed, Lizzy said, "I guess you're right. And anyway, he knows everyone."

Holly relaxed and finished her dinner, relieved that Lizzy wasn't going to withhold evidence. Mavis managed to snag a few more handouts, mostly ignoring Candy, who wanted to play. The kitten had little to no interest in people food. She had already eaten and was rolling around under Mavis and trying to get her attention by climbing on her back and swatting her ears.

"If he doesn't get here by the time we finish the dishes, we can take a walk. I feel bad Candy hasn't had much stimulation today."

"Okay by me. Maybe we can meet the lady staying in the fifth wheel."

"We should stay out of it. Somebody in that stack of photos is a murderer."

Lizzy narrowed her eyes. "What's going on with you? Do you just want to stay here indefinitely?"

Unable to explain, Holly shook her head and rose to clear the table. She had always let Lizzy take the lead and gave her plenty of leeway, understanding she had a creative brain and a lot of baggage. Together, however, they had a penchant for landing in trouble, and they were strangers in Serenity. *Should I call Jason?*

Lizzy grabbed a dish towel and began drying as Holly washed. "Are we having a fight?"

"Not unless you're mad at me for expressing my concerns."

"Not mad exactly, but puzzled. You've always been enthusiastic about ferreting out the bad guys and this time you're not."

"This time I'm scared."

Canting her head to one side, Lizzy gazed at her.

"You'll think it's silly, I suppose, but being surrounded by friends and family, knowing Jason's got my back, it makes a difference. We're alone here. If we get into trouble, we don't have anyone to help us."

"Like when I found Mrs. Crocker."

"I guess so. Were you afraid?"

"I was afraid when the intruder cut off my electricity in the middle of the night."

"But not when you found the body?"

"No—it didn't occur to me. I just wanted to know who killed her and why they did it in my house. Is that weird?"

Perhaps it was, but that's how Lizzy's brain worked. And here she was again, puzzling over whodunit instead of focusing on self-preservation.

⁕

Holly's silence screamed yes.

Maybe I am strange, but I can't help it. And there's something odd going on with the police. They might never catch the killer, and everyone knows murder is easier the second time. To Lizzy, that thought was a lot more terrifying than being among strangers.

She hung the dish towel to dry and said, "I'm going to take Mavis for a walk. Do you want to come?"

"You go ahead. I'll build a campfire."

Sticking her phone in her pocket and wrestling Mavis into her harness, Lizzy left the RV and headed toward the pool. The little dog seemed to sense her pensive mood and was especially vigilant, sniffing and barking at everything.

A tall, muscular man sat in front of a fire at the otherwise vacant party campsite. Lizzy thought she recognized him from some of Sal's photos and would have greeted him if not for his formidable scowl. As it was, he watched her pass with unfriendly eyes, intermittently poking the fire with a long stick.

Was he the drug dealer or the insurance scammer? Or both? Lizzy couldn't remember.

The next several sites were vacant, causing Lizzy to wonder if the police had halted both check-ins and check-outs during the investigation. That would have a major impact on the campground and the campers.

An enthusiastic bout of barking and tail wagging ensued when Mavis spotted a woman outside the fifth wheel. On her hands and knees, she sat back on her heels and tucked a strand of shiny brown hair behind her ear.

"She's just saying hello." Lizzy smiled.

"It's fine. She just startled me."

"Do you need any help?"

"No. I lost an earring the other day and thought it might have fallen out here, but I don't see it." She stood and brushed the dirt off her pant legs, then extended her hand. "I'm Darla, by the way. You're in the RV, aren't you?"

"Yes. I'm Lizzy. Nice to meet you." After shaking her hand, she asked, "Are the police making you extend your stay too?"

"No, I'm local." She paused. "I guess I can tell you." Looking to the left, then the right, as if someone might be eavesdropping, she continued. "I'm kind of hiding out from my husband right now. Sometimes he gets into these jealous rages, and he scares me.

"Does he hurt you?"

"Not so far, but my presence seems to set him off and he breaks things. Sometimes it's just better if I'm not at home."

"But if you're not home, doesn't that make him more paranoid?"

Darla chuckled without mirth. "It's a pattern we've been through many times. I disappear for a while and he drinks with his buddies down at the bar, then I go home, and he settles down for a bit."

"Well, Mavis and I should be on our way, but if you need help, or just someone to talk to, feel free to stop by. My friend Holly and I like company."

Chapter 12

The Seeker

Although ordinarily perceptive and aware of her surroundings, Lizzy allowed Mavis to lead her through the woods as she puzzled through everything she had learned since Sal's murder. At one point, the little dog stopped and began digging in the sand. *Sand?* Lizzy realized they were at the edge of the lake. The setting sun glinted off a small shiny object Mavis had unearthed. Glancing at Lizzy, she barked once and sat next to her treasure.

Lizzy squatted next to Mavis and picked up a gold earring with a dangling diamond, turning it over with long slender fingers. *Could this be what Darla was looking for?* "Good job, puppy." She put the earring in her pocket and noticed several pieces of thin broken glass. She placed the glass in her pocket as well and scanned the area. Remnants of crime-scene tape decorated the shore. Lingering streaks of orange and pink lay in the horizon, quickly disappearing as darkness set in. *We won't be able to get back without a flashlight.* The battery on her phone was at five percent and Holly didn't answer her call, so she sent her a text and sat to wait.

A gibbous moon hung low over the lake, its reflection throwing the clearing into shadow. Lizzy listened carefully. Bushes rustled before the sound of footsteps on gravel reached her. She moved quietly into the deeper shadows of the tree line, wishing to remain concealed. Her fearless dachshund, however, didn't understand the need for caution and began to bark. Survival instinct kicking in, Lizzy detached the leash from her harness and remained still as Mavis charged toward their unknown visitor. Almost immediately, she had second thoughts. *She's so small. I hope she doesn't get hurt.* Lizzy's heart pounded. *I shouldn't have let her loose. Murderers don't necessarily dislike dogs though. Did Holly send Garcia to find me?*

Mavis' ferocious-sounding barking continued, ending in a high-pitched yelp, then silence.

It took every ounce of Lizzy's self-control to remain where she was. She crouched at the base of a tree, wishing she had something to cover her bright hair. The seeker, as she thought of her unknown adversary, paced up and down the clearing, finally approaching the water's edge and turning on a flashlight. Lizzy studied the dark figure, trying to ascertain their identity. Age, sex, body type? Clothing? It was hard to tell, especially from a distance, but something about the shape and posture of the silhouette told her it was a man. *What's he looking for? The earring?*

Time slowed. The murderer, Lizzy assumed, was unhurried and methodical. He didn't find what he was looking for and finally gave up, heading for the trees. Mavis whined. *If you really do have ESP, stay quiet, puppy. I'll be there in a minute.* She forced herself to count out five minutes; then she slowly crawled toward the last place she heard Mavis. Unable to see, her progress was impeded by sharp twigs and stones that bruised her knees and scraped her hands.

Bushes rustled and twigs snapped. Lizzy lay flat. The seeker had been waiting. Does he know I'm here? Blinded by the beam of a flashlight, she squinted toward him as he located Mavis. The little dog snarled when he picked her up and the flashlight bobbed up and down, falling to the ground as he held on. Mavis was a master wiggler, seeming to squirm in every direction at once. Even with practice, Lizzy occasionally had difficulty carrying her when she wanted down.

Her entire body clenched when the seeker turned and carried Mavis into the tree line. *Where's he taking her? If he was going to hurt her, he would have done it here, wouldn't he?* She sat up and wondered what time it was. She was cold and sunrise was a long way off. *Should I try to walk back in the dark?* It might have been possible with Mavis, but on her own, she'd just get lost. *Mavis. Where are you? Please be okay.* She thought about her valiant little dog and felt guilty about her own cowardice.

She suspected the man who took Mavis was the murderer and was likely armed. Part of her wished she hadn't let Mavis loose, but another part of her realized if she hadn't, they might both be dead. *Please, God, if you're there, take care of Mavis and let her be okay.* Shivering violently, she stood and began a series of stretches.

More frightened than she had ever been, Holly packed an extra sweater and flashlight for Lizzy. She opened Lizzy's nightstand and contemplated the gun. *Should I take it?* She reached out with a shaky hand and picked it up. Lizzy told her it had a trigger guard. That's all she knew. She put it in her pocket and considered Mavis. Garcia and Quirk had found her hurt and without her leash. Holly doubted she'd be able to make the trek. "I'll be back soon, puppy. You take care of Candy."

She set the alarm and locked the RV. Switching on the flashlight, she began the long hike to the lake. Careful of her route, she moved slowly through the dark forest and jumped at every noise, each magnified by the silence; a cracking twig sounding like a gun shot. She remembered the deer. *They can probably be noisy.* Then she heard a long howl in the distance, and another, closer. She froze, listening carefully. Her heart raced. *A coyote?* She tried to move noiselessly, feeling danger all around her. The forest teemed with life that once heard couldn't be unheard. *I wonder what kinds of animals live here. Or maybe someone's following me.* She shivered.

When she could see the shimmering surface of the water ahead, she took a deep breath and called Lizzy's name. She stepped through the trees and into the clearing, calling louder. "Lizzy? Are you here?"

No answer. *Where did she go?* Holly walked toward the shore, then turned and scanned the dark tree line. She thought she saw movement and said, "Lizzy, I sure hope that's you."

"Are you here alone?"

"Yes. Where are you?"

"You walked all the way here by yourself?" Suddenly standing before her, Lizzy said, "I've never been so glad to see anyone in my life."

Holly hugged her fiercely. "You feel like ice." She took Lizzy's sweater out of her backpack and helped her into it.

"Why didn't you bring someone with you? Weren't you afraid?"

"Terrified." Her teeth chattered and she took the gun out of her pocket, handing it to Lizzy. "Garcia and Quirk went looking for you. They brought Mavis back and said they'd search again in the morning."

"Mavis! Is she okay?"

"Mostly."

"What does that mean?"

"She's limping a little and had some blood on her snout. I wasn't sure if it was hers."

"I've been so worried about her."

"She'll be fine."

"Didn't you get my text?"

"I did. That's why Garcia and Quirk were out looking for you."

"Weird." Lizzy canted her head.

"What happened here?"

Lizzy told her about the seeker.

"You don't know who it was?"

"No. I wonder if the police stayed together. Was the chief with them?"

"I didn't see him."

"Do you know the way back?"

"I think so. I brought an extra flashlight."

"Any idea what time it is?"

"Almost midnight."

"I'm sure glad you came. The thought of spending the night out here made me consider walking back in the dark."

The return trip was slow, but not as frightening. She wasn't alone. That helped. But being with Lizzy and the gun she never used gave Holly a sense of security. She knew her friend wasn't fearless; she had seen her fear firsthand when she moved to Harperstown. But her bravado, her willingness to put herself in danger despite the fear… she made Holly feel safer, braver even.

As they navigated the dark road, Lizzy didn't say much. *I wonder what she's thinking about.* Holly didn't want to intrude on her thoughts, but her curiosity finally got the best of her.

"I was just going over the people in those pictures and who knew where I went. I'm still not sure if he was looking for me, or something else."

How does it feel to always have such a busy brain? "Are you still upset with me?"

"You're currently my favorite person in the whole world."

"Okay, but I'm still asking."

"I'm not mad. Did you give them to Garcia?"

"I did, but I couldn't explain them like Helene did. He didn't seem very impressed."

"He'll probably go through them again in the morning. Did you tell him where we got them?"

"I had to."

"I guess that's okay. She said to do what we thought was best."

"Don't you trust him?"

"I'm not sure. Someone was in that clearing and whoever it was, came back for Mavis."

"He and Quirk were together though."

Lizzy didn't answer. Barking sounded from a distance and her pace quickened.

Holly tried to keep up, but she tripped and fell. Her flashlight hit the ground and went out.

Lizzy reached down to help her up. "Where's your flashlight?"

"I don't know. Somewhere around here."

Nearby bushes rustled and Lizzy spun around, shining her flashlight toward the sound. A pale face appeared in the beam of light and Holly screamed.

Two hands rose in the air. "Please. I'm sorry if I frightened you. I heard voices and came to see what was going on."

"Who are you?" Lizzy asked.

"My name's Leonard. I saw you earlier, walking your dog."

"From the party site."

"Yeah. Sorry about that. My cousin's idea."

"Well, no harm no foul. We'll get back to the RV now."

"Could I walk with you? My batteries died." He shook his flashlight.

"Okay."

They walked together in silence, and he thanked them before he veered toward his own campsite and disappeared into the darkness.

"Why did you let him walk back with us?" Holly asked.

"Two reasons. First, I'm pretty sure he's not the seeker. It was hard to judge size in the dark, but he's a burly guy."

"What's the second reason?"

"I don't know if he's dangerous and I figured it was safer knowing where he was. I thought if he was with us, he couldn't sneak up on us."

The moonlight glinted off Lizzy's toothy grin.

***

When Lizzy and Holly entered the motor home, Mavis rolled onto her back, tail wagging and pee squirting like a fountain. Lizzy scrunched her nose and laughed. She grabbed the little dog and carried her outside. "Poor baby. How long have you been holding that?" She set a wiggling Mavis down gently and rubbed her ears. "Finish your job and we'll get you something to eat... and a bath." She wrinkled her nose again.

The little red dog was so covered in dirt and sand she was brown. And she smelled of urine.

"I turned on the fireplace and made you some peach tea," Holly said through the cracked door.

"Ahh that sounds cozy. Thank you."

"Would you like a blanket?"

"No, I'll be fine. The sweater and the walk back warmed me up. Too bad we don't have a hot tub though." Lizzy grinned. She gently lifted Mavis and helped her back inside; then set her down and mixed her kibble with warm water to make a gravy.

"Didn't she eat already?"

"Sure, so did we, but I'm hungry again. It's been a stressful evening."

As soon as Lizzy's hand touched Mavis' head, she gobbled every bite, licking her empty bowl with gusto.

"She didn't even wait for the full doggy massage," Lizzy said in awe.

"Poor little thing had quite a night. Do you want something to snack on?"

"Silly question. Do we have any sweets?"

"Lots. What are you in the mood for?"

"Ice cream."

"I thought you were cold."

"It's toasty now—ohh s'mores! Can we make those inside? How about pizza?"

"You *are* hungry. Why don't you go take a hot shower and I'll make a pizza?"

"A giant one." Lizzy grinned. "Or two. Make two."

"You're a nut." Holly laughed.

The hot water stung like a thousand needles. It felt good on her sore muscles, but her scrapes and bruises made their presence known. She scrubbed Mavis clean and wrapped her in a towel before taking her own shower.

Mavis' big brown eyes watched her gingerly pat herself dry. She applied antibiotic ointment and bandages then dressed in loose shorty pajamas.

When she finally returned to the kitchen area with Mavis, Holly's eyebrows rose at the dozens of bandages. Lizzy was focused on the pizza.

"There's a piece missing." She sat at the table.

"I can't imagine how that happened. Mavis? Did you do that?"

"Aurooherer."

"I might believe you if she wasn't hurt." Lizzy picked up a slice and took a bite. "This is your best one yet."

"It's exactly the same. I think you're just hungry."

"I am."

"Me too. All that extra exercise. There's another in the oven."

Mavis sat at their feet, focused on the table, but her heart wasn't in it. Her eyes closed briefly, and she wobbled. Candy was sleeping on the upholstered bench next to Holly. "I need to get Mavis to bed. She's asleep on her feet."

"Are you full?"

"Maybe one more slice. I'll probably be sorry later."

"We can always have leftovers tomorrow."

Reluctantly leaving the table, Lizzy scooped Mavis up and carried her into the bedroom. She got into bed and felt the little dog's breathing change before she arranged the bedding. Unlike Mavis, however, Lizzy lay with her eyes open, revisiting that evening's events. She remembered her prayer on the beach, her first one ever. *Thank you, God, for keeping her safe. I love her so much.* She turned onto her side and wrapped her arms around Mavis, pulling her close.

Ferocious barking woke her, of course. It wasn't Mavis' *I need to go outside* barking. She stood stiff-legged on the bed, in guard-dog mode.

Lizzy groaned. "I was hoping we could sleep in this morning."

The insistent barking continued.

"Okay, I'm up." She stood and glanced in the mirror mounted on the closet door. Her hair was wilder than usual. "Whatever," she muttered, running her hand through it and making it worse. "Come on, puppy."

Mavis looked at her and whined.

"Leg still bothering you?" Lizzy gently placed her on the floor, then opened the bedroom door.

Mavis dashed to the front door as Holly closed it. "I'm sorry. I asked them to come back later so you could sleep."

"Who? The police?"

"Yeah. They were worried about you. Quirk said I should have called last night. Actually, he said I shouldn't have gone out alone. But I think they were relieved that I found you."

Lizzy eyed her long, tangled hair and silky pink housecoat. "Are you going back to bed?"

"No, I'm up now. You can though."

"Nah. I'm awake. Maybe we can take a nap later. I'll take Mavis out. Do you think her leg's okay?"

"It obviously hurts, but it's not broken. You don't have any idea what happened to her?"

"I couldn't see but her yelp sounded like when Theo kicked her. She didn't get back up or come to me, so maybe she was stunned."

Candy meowed from the loft.

"I guess it's past breakfast time." Holly reached up for the kitten. "Why don't we get dressed and I'll make French toast?"

"Sounds great."

"Are you hungry Mavis?"

"Ahrooherer." Mavis wagged her tail and licked Candy's ear.

Chapter 13

Mrs. Gross

Shivering in the crisp, morning air, Lizzy pulled her sweater close and urged Mavis to hurry. She gave her an assist on the steps when they returned and sighed happily at the warmth and the scent of cinnamon. "Is it my imagination, or has it been colder the last day or two?"

"I think it has." Holly plated two pieces of French toast and put two more in the pan. "Are you ready for these?"

"Yes, yes, yes!" Lizzy slathered the bread with butter and natural maple syrup, heaping berries on top. "Can I have seconds?" she asked, cutting a square and sticking it in her mouth. "Oops." She patted her chin with a napkin. "I might have put a little too much syrup."

Holly giggled. "You're so fun to cook for." She placed her own breakfast on a plate and added more to the pan before sitting at the table with Lizzy. Two bites in, Mavis glanced at the door and barked.

"You eat. I'll answer the door and turn the toast." Lizzy rose. "Toast first." She detoured to the stove as the knock sounded. Mavis was rarely mistaken.

Darla Gross stood at the bottom of the steps, her eyes red and swollen. "You said I could come if I needed anything." She sniffed.

"Of course. Come in. What happened?" Lizzy held the door for her. "Have you eaten?"

"No, but I don't want to interrupt your breakfast."

"Have a seat. You might as well join us." Lizzy caught the French toast just in time and added two more. "Holly, this is Darla. She's staying in the fifth wheel."

"Glad to meet you."

She accepted the plate Lizzy handed her. "This looks delicious."

"Would you like some coffee?" Lizzy asked.

"Yes please." Darla hiccupped.

Lizzy turned the toast and grabbed her own plate, placing the second batch on top of the first, which was already cold. Finally, she sat and took a bite, groaning at the goodness.

Darla ate in silence.

"I'm sorry. What happened to you? Is it your husband?"

"Go ahead and eat first. This is too good to ruin with my tales of woe."

"I didn't even know I liked French toast until I met Holly. I think she has a secret ingredient."

Silence loomed as the three women finished their breakfast. Even Mavis was quiet as she stared at the table. Lizzy set her fork down and patted her flat stomach. "I wish I had enough room for more."

Holly giggled.

"I'm glad I came," Darla said. "Thank you for breakfast. Being here with the two of you somehow makes everything seem a little more normal."

Holly tilted her head like a little bird.

"I have a special friend who stays with me sometimes. The police came over this morning and arrested him for murder."

"But…" Lizzy didn't want to say too much because she knew more than she had let on.

"They said they have evidence, but the victim was my friend's son. Who would kill their own son? And he's a policeman. Do they think he suddenly lost his mind?"

"Did he have a motive?"

"I don't think so. I guess *I* did but I didn't tell him."

"What didn't you tell him?"

Darla looked at Lizzy with wide blue eyes. "I probably shouldn't say."

She gazed at her for another moment then continued, speaking more quickly, like she had to let it out. "Sal tried to blackmail me. I guess he might have tried with his father too, but I don't think he had the guts."

"Officer Garcia is supposed to come by later so we can try to find out about the evidence."

"You won't tell him, will you? About the blackmail?"

"No. He's coming to talk to me about getting lost in the woods last night."

Darla had gradually torn her paper napkin into tiny pieces as she spoke. "I've been so worried, and I can't go see him. He'd be angry if I caused his wife any embarrassment."

"Maybe he should have thought about that before he started having an affair," Holly mumbled.

"It was an accident." Darla stood. "I should go."

"I'll let you know if we hear anything," Lizzy said.

"She's only about my age," Holly said when she left. "I wonder what *accidentally* caused her to have an affair with the chief."

"No idea. But she told me she's hiding out from her husband, so maybe he was just supportive when she needed a shoulder."

Day four in Texas. Holly watched Mavis trot back and forth behind Lizzy as she paced the length of the motor home. Ordinarily she would bake, but the kitchen was full of sweets. Lizzy would write, but she wasn't for some reason. Both of them were bored and cooped up without their usual outlets.

"Let's go outside and make a campfire."

"Okay." Lizzy sighed.

"You don't want to?"

"I don't mind. I'll bring the marshmallows."

Holly built the fire and sat in her camp chair.

"Why haven't you been writing?"

"I'm stuck and I can't concentrate because of—" she threw her arms out in an all-encompassing gesture.

"What are you stuck on?"

"I don't want to talk about it, if that's okay. Let's talk about the investigation."

Holly nodded. "You went to see Darla yesterday."

"Yeah." Lizzy didn't mention the earring. *Should I give it to Garcia?*

"What do we have so far?"

"The photos, the boots, the chief and whatever evidence they found, the seeker, whoever that was, and whatever he was looking for."

"Who are the suspects?"

"Process of elimination? We can probably leave out Helene, Sal's mom, Freida, Quirk, Garcia, and Darla. And probably the policewoman who was at the crime scene. I don't know anything about her."

"Why Darla?"

"Two things. First, it seemed like a physical murder, right? Whoever did it had to hit the victim with something, then move the body. Second, I'm guessing the murderer and the seeker are the same person, and I'm fairly certain the seeker was a man."

"So, a man who was in one of those pictures?"

"The chief, Jim, the scowling guy, the football coach, the guys who tried to break into the RV. Anyone else?"

"Who's the scowling guy?"

"He's the one who walked back with us last night. Leonard? He's either the drug dealer or the insurance scammer. I got them mixed up. Maybe he's both."

Mavis barked hysterically, jumping against the side of her pen when Officer Garcia pulled up in his cruiser.

"What's going on, Mavis?"

Afraid she would do further damage to her leg, Lizzy lifted her from the pen and struggled to hold on through her violent contortions.

She returned Garcia's wave before heading inside.

Placing Mavis in her crate with her favorite treats, she didn't know what was wrong but felt guilty leaving her by herself. If it was anyone other than the police, she would have asked them to leave.

Chapter 14

Updates

Outside, Garcia perched on a log across from Holly. The dark circles under his eyes and his rumpled uniform were at odds with his friendly smile.

"Sorry about that," Lizzy said. "Was it you who found Mavis last night?"

"Quirk found her, but he made me pick her up because she was…" He shook his head. "I don't know if she was scared, or hurt, or what, but she really didn't want anyone touching her."

She glanced toward the motor home, where she could hear Mavis' continued barking inside.

"How did you find Lizzy?" Garcia asked.

Lizzy gave Holly an almost imperceptible shake of her head, so she said, "I just walked toward the lake, calling. She had tripped and twisted her ankle."

"I think I must have fallen asleep," Lizzy added. "Holly's voice sounded like a dream."

Deep lines appeared across Garcia's otherwise youthful forehead. "I wish you would have told us you planned to go out by yourself. That could have been dangerous."

"I was worried when you gave up looking for her."

Garcia took a deep breath and let it out with a sigh. "We had to get back to the station. The chief has been arrested. He was off last night and might have been out here looking for a missing uniform button."

"Why do you think that?" *Could the chief have been the seeker?* Lizzy thought back and tried to remember exactly what she had observed. She had only seen the chief once.

"We found the button earlier and searched the uniforms hanging in his office. One of his shirts had a missing button and a blood stain on the back shoulder."

Lizzy thought about that for a moment. "How long have you worked with him? Is he the type of person who could kill his own son?"

"I hate to think it, but the evidence is strong. He had motive and opportunity."

"What about the other people in those pictures?"

"Like who?"

"The couple who scammed the insurance company? The drug dealer? The football coach? Have you checked everyone's alibis?"

"I'll ask Quirk about them."

Lizzy wasn't at all sure about Quirk. She decided not to mention the earring.

"If nothing changes, you should be free to leave in a day or two."

As soon as Garcia left, the barking ceased. Lizzy glanced at the RV again. "She really hates him."

"Is it him, or the association?" Holly asked. "Remember how she was with Dave?"

"I thought of that. Sometimes I wish I could read her mind."

"Do you think the chief might have been the person by the lake last night?"

"It's possible. I don't know what to say to Darla."

"Well think fast because here she comes."

"I'll let Mavis out." Lizzy went inside and unlocked the crate.

The little dog sat and stared at her reproachfully.

"I know. I'm sorry. We needed to hear what he had to say. You can come out now."

Lizzy reached into the crate to pull her out, but she backed into the corner.

"Suit yourself. We'll be outside." She walked toward the door and Mavis followed.

Holly and Darla turned when she emerged.

Placing Mavis in the pen with Candy, Lizzy tried to marshal her thoughts.

"What did he say?" Darla asked.

"He didn't tell us not to talk about it," Holly said.

"That might be because he thinks we don't know anyone." Lizzy paused. "You know the chief and we don't so let's share information and see what we can come up with."

Darla shifted her weight on the log she sat on and wrung her hands.

"Officer Garcia said they found a uniform button at the lake and blood on the chief's shirt."

"He couldn't have killed Sal. He loved him more than anyone. Not only that, he has a deep respect for upholding the law. He just wouldn't."

Lizzy told her about the muddy boots. "How could someone have gotten access to his uniform shirt?"

"I don't know. His wife? She acts so sweet, but he says she can be malicious."

"Can I show you some photos?" Lizzy opened the gallery app on her phone.

"You took pictures of them?" Holly asked.

Nodding, Lizzy passed the phone to Darla, whose eyes widened as she scrolled. "Where did you get these?"

"Sal left them with a lady named Helene."

"That makes sense."

"Do any of them mean anything to you?"

Darla scrolled quickly and then abruptly stopped and straightened her spine. "She's supposed to be dead."

"Who?"

Darla stood. "I have to check on something. This could change everything."

She sat on the floor, staring at the wall. Bereft, her grief made it difficult to breathe. Patricia had never thought too much about her feelings for Sal, but she suspected she loved him. Her only friend, her confidant; he was gone.

The photos he left with her lay on the floor, mocking her. She realized she needed to do something, but she didn't know what. She sucked in air and stared at the wall some more.

Random memories of their time together, their conversations, floated through her mind, some evoking a smile, others tears. She thought of how they met, how Sal always stood up for her, of him picking her up and dusting her off after their cruel classmates pushed her off the monkey bars. He was her hero, and she had thought him invincible.

Sitting up straighter, she thought of another person he protected. He bought her a dog when she was worried about her safety. *What kind of person bullies a ninety-year-old woman?* She frowned, then gave her head a shake. *Helene. I should visit Helene. She's the one person who'll understand.*

Downstairs, she found her mother sitting at the kitchen table with a cup of tea. "Are you doing okay?"

Patricia nodded. Her mother, Wanda, had been the one to deliver the news of Sal's murder with the excitement and gusto of a juicy piece of gossip.

"I'm sorry I was so tactless, honey. I didn't mean to be insensitive; I just didn't think."

"I know, Mom. It's okay," Patricia said, her face carefully masking her emotions.

"Oh. I almost forgot. Jim's going to stay with us for a few days. Something about needing to do some work on his van."

Great. Icing on the cake. "I'm going to go see Helene. I'll be back in a while." She knew her mother well and left quickly to avoid the emotional drama getting ready to unfold.

* * *

Lizzy paced. "I need to walk."

"Would you like company?"

"No, I'll just take Mavis if that's okay."

"Is it safe?"

"I think so. I'll take my gun."

"Have you ever used it?"

"No, but I know how."

"Be careful."

Holly sat and watched Lizzy walk away. *This is my chance to bake. What should I make? Something we can eat for dinner. Quiche. Two of them.* She smiled to herself. *The walk will make her hungry.*

She switched on the radio and began efficiently retrieving utensils and ingredients from cupboards and drawers. Candy, bored, clawed her way up Holly's pantleg, so she placed the kitten on her shoulder and washed her hands again.

The simple crust took only ten minutes to prep and twenty to chill in the freezer, but Holly only had one pan. She took her time and made them separately.

Two hours later, Lizzy still hadn't returned. Candy, having long since tired of her shoulder perch, slept on the sofa. *Should I be worried?*

Cutting herself a slice of quiche, she sat at the table and took a bite. *Delicious.* She smiled. *Lizzy will love this.* The savory cheese and tangy artichoke hearts were a perfect combination.

After she ate, she went outside and added wood to the smoldering embers of the fire. She left the RV door open, with just the screen door closed so she could hear the radio and Candy if she wanted out. *We've been together so much I've forgotten how to be alone,* she thought, vaguely worried about Lizzy's prolonged absence. *No, this is different.* She missed Barker and her clinic, her parents, even Jason. *I want to go home.*

By the time Lizzy returned, Holly had worked herself into a state. She looked at her friend and burst into tears.

"What happened?"

"N-nothing. I just—I want to go home."

"I don't think I can cancel this late, but you could fly back if you want."

Lizzy's words shocked her out of her maudlin bout of self-pity. She had completely forgotten where they were headed and why. "No, I'm sorry. We have to get to LA. It'll be better once we get out of here."

"I feel really bad. I wanted you to get away and have a good time."

"Not your fault."

"You did say I keep finding bodies."

"And you pointed out it was Mavis."

Hearing her name, she wriggled to get down.

"Is she okay?"

"I think so. Her limp got worse, and I had to carry her most of the way back. She's surprisingly heavy."

Mavis whined.

"I bet you're thirsty."

"And hungry." Holly giggled. "Speaking of which, I made quiche."

"I don't know if I like quiche." Lizzy's stomach gurgled.

"You'll love it."

Chapter 15

Arrest

Once she had eaten copious amounts of quiche and showered, Lizzy joined Holly outside by the fire. "I'm not usually bored, but this whole camping thing gets really old."

"I think we've got it too easy. Part of the fun is catching fish to eat, cooking over the fire, setting up our tents, hiking to the shower room or rinsing off in the lake. With the RV we don't have to do any of that stuff."

"I guess."

"Plus, we usually camp for a few days, not a week."

"I wonder if the managers are back. They might have some bikes or fishing gear we can rent."

"Or maybe we can sneak back into the pool." Holly giggled.

"I did enjoy the pool. What are we going to do tonight?"

"Let's watch a movie. We have popcorn."

They ended up watching *Agatha Raisin* reruns, laughing over the title of the first episode, "The Quiche of Death." Lizzy was enchanted by the main character, played by Ashley Jensen, but she was extremely tired and unused to watching television. She fell asleep during the third episode and dreamt of the vicar's wife, who helped her solve Sal's murder. An idea woke her, but she forgot what it was before she could write it down.

Holly snored softly in the loft bed and Mavis sat in front of the door, thumping her tail.

"Hold on puppy. I'll take you out in a sec."

Outside, Mavis rooted around and barked at a gentle breeze that soughed through the old-growth trees. Lizzy thought about the night before and shivered. *I don't like this place. Something's wrong here.*

"I need to teach you to sleep in," Lizzy mumbled the next morning, covering her head with her pillow.

Apparently feeling better, Mavis jumped on her and burrowed her snout under the pillow, her long tongue licking Lizzy's face.

"Eww. Sto-opp. Go away."

More face licking. Lizzy threw her covers aside and sat up. "You're a naughty dog."

The scent of bacon wafted under the bedroom door. *That's why she's bugging me.* The clock read seven.

Holly stood in the kitchen area sipping coffee and turning the bacon with a fork. "I knew this would lure you out of bed."

"It might have, eventually, but Mavis was impatient. I need coffee. How I can be sleep deprived on vacation is beyond me."

"Mavis has a strong internal clock."

"Very true. Let's go outside then I'll give you breakfast, you rascal."

Tail wagging, Mavis ran toward the door, then back to the stove. She focused her big brown eyes on Lizzy and whined.

"Come on. We'll be back before it's even ready."

Mavis didn't dawdle. She was momentarily distracted by a squirrel but quickly took care of business and ran for the door.

Lizzy fed both pets and poured herself another cup of coffee. "What's for breakfast?"

"Omelets. And bacon of course."

"Fancy." Lizzy set the table and carried their plates the few feet from the stove.

Mavis stared intently as she stuck a piece of bacon in her mouth.

"Roherer."

"Do you really think you deserve bacon?"

Dancing on her hind legs, Mavis barked.

"Well, you don't." Lizzy broke off a piece and offered it to her.

Holly sat across the table and picked up her fork. "I was craving vegetables."

"Delicious."

"I don't know how you can even taste it."

Lizzy looked at her plate. "It's just Tapatio. I can still taste it." She shook the bottle a few more times.

Mavis growled, then ran to the door, barking, and Lizzy stood. "You know, for being strangers here, we sure get a lot of company. Finish your omelet. I'll stall whoever it is." She winked, then let herself out. Mavis, barking ferociously, sounded like she was body slamming the door.

Garcia stood outside, accompanied by Quirk. "I tried to wait until after breakfast," he mumbled. "Could you secure your dog?"

"Yes. I'll be right back." Lizzy went back inside and closed the door.

"It's Garcia again. He wants me to clear the way." She picked up her noisy, squirming dog and carried her into the bedroom.

"I know this is upsetting, but it's just for a few minutes. You be a good girl."

Mavis lunged at the door, barking. For once, she wasn't wagging her tail.

Holly finished her breakfast as Lizzy ushered the officers inside, noting the change in Garcia's demeanor. He stood stiffly, refusing her offer of coffee. Something was different about Quirk too, but she couldn't pinpoint what it was.

"Holly Schneider, I'm arresting you for the murder of Salamander Elkhurst," Garcia began. "You have the right to remain silent—"

Lizzy interrupted. "You know she was with me all morning. How could she have killed him?"

"If I were you, I wouldn't emphasize that stance.

"You might end up sharing a cell." His lips formed a straight line. Uncompromising. "May I proceed?"

Shocked, she stared at him then watched as he cuffed Holly unnecessarily and led her outside. Quirk remained silent.

"Call Jason," Holly said. She appeared calm, but Lizzy knew she wasn't. As for Lizzy, she was furious. After they drove off, she kicked the wall, then hopped around on one foot, wishing she hadn't. All thoughts of breakfast gone, she hobbled to the bedroom door and released Mavis, who looked at her like she was Benedict Arnold. She decided to forgive her, however, after Lizzy gave her the remainder of her omelet.

Closing her eyes, she tried to still her mind and her emotions. She didn't want to call Jason, but she didn't know what else to do. *I'm Holly's alibi and if I get locked up too, we won't have anyone to help us.* She opened her phone and stared at Jason's number. She chewed on her bottom lip. Finally, with a deep breath she dialed, completely deflated when it went to voicemail.

"This is Lizzy," she said. "We need your help. Please call me back."

She disconnected and set the phone down; then rose and paced. Mavis followed on her heels and whined. "It's okay, puppy. We'll get her out somehow." She sat at her laptop and Googled law enforcement in Texas. She had heard about the Rangers and wondered if they could be of assistance.

Startled by her blaring ring tone, she placed her hand on her chest for a second before answering Jason's return call. She told him everything that had happened, ending with Holly's arrest and her research.

"I can't come until tomorrow, but I'll be there as soon as I can. How will I find you?"

"We're in a small town east of Dallas, called Serenity, in a campground of the same name. I haven't been out of the campground, so I don't know what the town is like."

"I'll call you when I'm on my way. Just relax and stay safe."

* · ·◁⊂◇⊃▷· ·*

After he spoke with Lizzy, Jason's first impulse was to drive directly to the airport and hop on the next flight, but he had obligations. He left the hospital where he had been interviewing a man who had been involved in a bar fight and drove to the police station.

Barker glanced up from his desk when he entered. "What's going on? You look... agitated."

"I need to fly to Dallas tomorrow morning. Holly's been arrested. Can you cover for me for a few days?"

Barker stood and opened his mouth to speak, but Jason said, "I know you want to go, but I have to do this. You'll see her next week."

Frowning, Barker resumed his seat. "I don't see why you get to go."

"Lizzy called me and asked." He didn't mention he was the boss.

"What about Harvey?"

"I'll leave him with my mom." Jason thought he'd better make sure that was okay. Even though she loved the enormous German shepherd, she and his dad might have plans.

"Can't we both go?"

"I know it's tough, but we just don't have enough manpower. We can't leave Nettle on his own. What if something happens?"

Barker sighed.

"Don't worry. I'll take care of it." Jason, his heart thudding against his ribcage, walked into his office and picked up the phone. Although he was worried about his sister, he was equally excited to see Lizzy. *Is that wrong?* He thought maybe it was, but he couldn't help it.

Chapter 16

A Waiting Game

Helene smiled at the knock on her door until she remembered it wasn't Salamander. Lucky walked with her to answer and sat politely waiting for her to indicate whether her visitor should be treated with respect.

A stranger stood on the porch, pale and expressionless.

They stared at each other in silence before the stranger said, "I'm sorry. I'm Salamander's friend, Patricia. He spoke of you so often I forgot we haven't met."

"Come in, dear."

"He told me about Lucky too," her voice quavered, and she looked away, at the dog, holding her hand out for him to sniff.

Helene's heart ached for the girl. She closed the door behind her and said, "Come on into the kitchen. It's where we always had our best conversations." She got Patricia settled at the table, with coffee and lemon bars, then sat across from her.

"Lemon bars." Patricia smiled wanly. "He always said yours were his favorite."

"Go ahead and try one." Helene watched as she took a bite and chuckled as the powdered sugar sprayed everywhere.

"Delicious but messy. Could I have a napkin?"

"I should've warned you."

"I hope you don't mind me stopping by like this." Patricia's voice shook slightly as she brushed some of the powdered sugar off her T-shirt.

"Not at all, dear. Did you just need to talk?"

"That and something else. I thought you might be the only one who understands.

"The loss. I feel like the bottom has fallen out of my world."

"Yes, I understand."

"Now my brother's come to stay and I'm afraid he might have had something to do with Sal's death. He never comes home, even for dinner."

"Who's your brother?"

"Jim. He and his friends made our lives miserable when we were kids."

"Salamander spoke of him."

"There's another thing though. Sal left something with me, and I don't know what to do with it."

"Snapshots?"

Patricia nodded. "He said he left most of them with you, but didn't want to get you involved with these." She pulled out a small packet and passed it across the table.

Slowly opening the packet, Helene drew the pictures out and studied them. "I was afraid of something like this," she said.

⁂

At the station, Holly wasn't processed. She wasn't interviewed. She was placed in a cell and ignored. The lack of windows made it difficult to tell what time it was, and her insomnia kicked in so she couldn't sleep. The omelet she had for breakfast tided her over for a while, but eventually she began to feel hungry. Her stomach rumbled, reminding her of Lizzy. *I hope she's okay.*

Although confused about her situation and uncomfortable in the small cell, she wasn't afraid. She had no doubt Lizzy had called Jason and help was on the way. With nothing to do but think, she considered their friendship. They had only met three months ago, and Lizzy was complicated, but Holly trusted her implicitly. Jason thought she was reckless, but it wasn't recklessness.

When someone Lizzy cared about was in need, she leapt into action with no consideration for her own wellbeing. She thought about how Lizzy had stood between her and a murderer with a gun. She had raced into Holly's burning clinic to rescue her patients from the fire. She had planned this trip, even though it involved facing her greatest fear. Holly loved and admired her, but she worried about her too. Worse than sitting in a jail cell was the thought of what Lizzy might be up to. *I hope Jason gets here soon.*

⁂

That evening, Officer Garcia showed up at the motor home. He smiled kindly when Lizzy opened the door and held up a six-pack of beer. "I thought you might need a shoulder," he said.

"Are you kidding me?" Mavis barked and snarled behind the closed screen door.

Garcia's smile disappeared. "I was just following orders this morning. Don't you want to know why Holly was arrested?"

"Yes, I do, but don't pretend it's a social call."

"Whatever." He shrugged. "I was just being friendly."

"So, why was she arrested?"

"How about you invite me in, and we have a beer?"

"I don't think so. Come back with another officer and we can talk." Lizzy closed and locked the door and set the alarm before sitting on the sofa. Mavis continued to bark until he drove away.

Lizzy's fury had returned with Garcia's visit. He had been so cold and threatening that morning, when he arrested Holly. Then he arrived with beer, in uniform and driving a police cruiser, as if nothing had happened. She felt physically sick. *I can't believe I recommended him to Jason. What was he thinking? Is he any smarter than Quirk? I hope Jason can help because they don't seem to have any idea what they're doing.*

It had been a long day, and the night stretched out before her.

Never one to pause when someone needed a hand, she found the waiting unbearable. She remembered Holly's words when they argued. *'We're alone here. If we get into trouble, we don't have anyone to help us.'*

Lizzy had been on her own since she was sixteen. She'd never had anyone to rely on. But she was beginning to understand. Since moving to Harperstown, she'd made real friends. She had a support system. And since Holly got arrested, her words took on a greater meaning.

Chapter 17

Leonard to the Rescue

Lizzy left the bedroom door open that night and to her surprise, Mavis and Candy let her sleep in. She woke at eight to find them tearing up packages in the pantry.

"How did you get that door open?"

Mavis, covered in flour, wagged her tail without a sign of guilt. Candy nonchalantly groomed a paw.

She poked a toe at the mess. "Augh. Incorrigible. Do you need to go outside?"

Prancing to the door, Mavis barked twice. Lizzy grabbed a damp wash cloth on her way out and once the little dog took care of business, she removed the majority of the flour from her coat. Mavis stood with her front paws on the steps and whined, anxious to continue her destruction.

"I don't think so," Lizzy said. "You're going to explode."

Tall and narrow, with larger items on the bottom, the pantry provided the perfect playground for the mischievous dachshund and her sidekick. Mavis had discovered her dog food along with crackers, a box of cereal, a bag of flour, and other dry goods. Lizzy placed the mangled packages in a garbage bag and swept the floor before starting a pot of coffee, then considered whether she should give the animals breakfast. *Who knows how much they've already eaten, especially Mavis.* Deciding to err on the side of caution, Lizzy prepared their food as usual. Candy was easy, but Mavis required a little warm water to make a gravy and some pets. Lizzy massaged the little dog's ears, head, and neck, then stepped back and watched her eat. Her pantry snack didn't appear to have affected her appetite.

Her morning routine disrupted, Lizzy looked at the closed pantry door and sighed.

The remaining cleanup vied for attention with the rumble of her empty stomach. *It can wait.* She removed the left-over quiche from the refrigerator. Unsure whether to heat it or not, she ate one slice cold while she heated another, deciding she liked it better cold.

Even after her super-sized breakfast, Mavis sat and begged, but Lizzy ignored her, absorbed in her thoughts. After breakfast, she decided she should spend a little time with Candy. She built a small fire outside and, placing Mavis in her pen, sat in the camp chair with the kitten and her coffee. Candy had other ideas. She wanted to play in the pen.

Lizzy went back inside to refill her coffee, then sat staring at nothing. She puzzled over why Holly had been arrested and how she was doing. Then she wondered if Darla could give her a ride into town and what it was she had wanted to check on the previous morning.

She sat up with purpose. "Want to go for a walk, puppy? I need some exercise."

Putting a harness on a wiggling dachshund is like trying to hold onto a floundering fish. "Cut it out, Mavis." The little dog rolled onto her back, still wiggling. "Ha. Gotcha." Lizzy slid the harness under her and pulled her little legs through the holes. Once she fastened the clasp, she flipped her over and clipped on the leash. "Little nut. If anyone saw this performance, they'd think you didn't want to go."

Mavis looked up at Lizzy and wagged her tail. "We'll be right back, Candy. You be good."

She started in the opposite direction. Strolling leisurely, she allowed her mind to pick at recent events. *Why would they release the chief? It sounded like they had a strong case against him. And why Holly? Because she's from out of town? Even if they considered the photos evidence, Sal had mistaken her identity. We need an advocate the police will listen to. Will Jason be able to make them see sense?*

Before she knew it, Lizzy had reached the fifth wheel. She stopped and knocked on the door, but no one answered.

She waited a moment and tried again, then gave up and continued her walk. Mavis examined the bushes next to the road. Bees and butterflies alighted on tiny flowers and a squirrel froze at their presence before darting up a thick trunk.

The jarring roar of an engine startled her. "Run!" a male voice rang out. Lizzy lifted Mavis by her harness and held her close, glancing over her shoulder as she took two long strides into the brush. A man sprinted toward her with his arms extended in front of him as a Jeep raced in their direction. His hands connected with her hips, propelling her further off the road.

She held Mavis above her head as the ground rushed toward her face. In a painful rendition of the famous *Pete Rose* dive, Lizzy slid to a halt on her belly. Dirt in her mouth and stinging from head to toe, she lay stunned for a moment. The first to recover, Mavis trotted toward her and nudged one of her arms with a whine.

"I'm okay, puppy. Give me a sec." She rolled over and sat up slowly, scanning the area for the man who had possibly saved her life. He lay crumpled in a heap, about twelve feet away.

She crawled toward him and studied his face. It was the perpetually scowling man from the party campsite, Leonard. His eyes moved in her direction, and he groaned.

"What was that?" she asked. "Can you move?"

"Somebody doesn't like you." He wheezed. "I think my leg is broken."

Darla ran toward them from the fifth wheel. "I saw what happened. Should I call for an ambulance?"

"Yes," Lizzy said.

"I'm sorry I didn't answer the door. I was changing." Darla dialed 911 with shaky hands and gave the dispatcher their location.

"Did you see who it was?" the man asked.

"No. I know the car, but the driver was wearing a ski mask."

"You know the car?" Lizzy repeated.

"It was mine," she whispered. "They aimed right at you."

"I'm glad you're here with us. There won't be any question." The man rolled his eyes back toward Lizzy. "I'm Leonard. We met last night. Sorry about the shove."

"No. Thank you. You saved my life." *Why did he do that? I need to get into town.* "Would you mind if I ride with you to the hospital?"

"We should probably stick together for a bit. Things are getting out of hand."

"What do you mean?"

Leonard closed his eyes and grimaced.

"Could you get my phone number to Helene?" Lizzy asked Darla. "I need to talk to her."

Darla nodded. "Is this about Mary?"

"Partly, maybe. I'll find out." Leonard's ominous frown gave Lizzy shivers.

"Could you watch Mavis while I'm gone?"

"Of course." Darla held out her arms.

Surprisingly, Mavis went to her and licked her cheek. "What a sweet doggy. We'll have lots of fun together."

The ambulance pulled up, lights flashing. Two EMTs loaded Leonard onto a stretcher and agreed to let Lizzy accompany him.

<hr>

Lizzy texted Jason her new location and was surprised to find Helene waiting outside the hospital when the ambulance arrived. She ordered the nursing staff to take them to a private room and to locate the on-call doctor.

Lizzy gaped.

"Close your mouth, young lady. I'm President of the Board. They do what they're told."

She closed her mouth and followed the gurney to a spacious white room that glowed from the sunlight pouring through the window.

"Now, what's this all about, Leonard?" Helene demanded.

"I saw this lady walking her dog, then I heard someone rev their engine and saw Darla's Jeep racing toward her. I yelled, trying to warn her and ran, but when I pushed her out of the Jeep's path, it swerved and caught my leg. I felt like I was flying and then I wasn't."

"Is Darla safe?"

"I don't rightly know. She saw them pictures and came to talk to me."

Helene tapped a papery cheek with her index finger.

The doctor entered the room, and she stayed with Lizzy while he took Leonard away for x-rays.

"Where's your friend?"

"They've arrested her for Sal's murder."

One eyebrow rose. "How absurd."

"More absurd than arresting the police chief?"

At odds with the situation, the miniscule, sly smile on Helene's face was so fleeting that Lizzy wondered if she had imagined it.

Gazing at her, as if making a decision, Helene finally said, "Most of us here in Serenity are related, one way or the other. And family loyalty runs deep. Now, that's usually a good thing, but it can get dangerous when you're dealing with power and things that aren't quite black and white."

Not sure what she was getting at, Lizzy remained silent.

"Lately, something's been growing here, like a weed. Someone's been taking the law into their own hands. I tried to warn Sal, but he wasn't listening." Helene pressed her lips together and closed her eyes. "Such a dear boy."

Or not such a dear, if he was blackmailing people. "Do you suspect anyone in particular?"

A radiologist wheeled Leonard back into the room and Helene clamped her mouth shut. Following the radiologist, the doctor said, "He's fractured his leg in three places and needs pins. We'll have to operate."

Lizzy stood in the corner while Helene quizzed the doctor carefully, then the old woman sat with Leonard and spoke in hushed tones. She finally stood and he said, "Yes, Gran." Patting his hand, she turned to leave, giving Lizzy a final nod.

"Will you be safe?"

"I have a dog that's bigger than me and a shotgun. I'll be just fine." She marched from the room like she owned the place. Perhaps she did.

"Is she *your* grandmother too?"

"Yeah." His eyes drooped and he slurred a bit.

"She did say everyone around here was related."

"Yeah. Sleepy." His eyes closed.

"They gave you pain meds?"

"Mhm." His head bobbed up and down.

"When Helene gave me Sal's photos, she explained why everyone could be a suspect, including you. Why would she do that? I wouldn't have known the difference."

"She probably wanted whoever you went to, to know that you knew."

"But Holly gave them to Garcia and couldn't remember the explanations."

"An' she's in jail." He snored softly.

"Wait. What's that mean? Hey. Wake up." She sat in a chair across the room and studied Leonard's face. The medication-induced sleep erased the signs of pain and stress from his face, making him look like a softer younger version of himself. Inside the room, only the beeps from the monitors broke the silence, but she could hear voices and the bustle of the ward through the thin walls.

She thought about Leonard. He had seemed angry and menacing, sitting by the fire. His picture was among Sal's potential blackmail victims. But he had saved her life and was apparently related to Helene. He was friendly with Darla. *Who is he really? He wouldn't have put his life at risk to save me if he was a bad guy. Would he? Why did he save me?*

Chapter 18

Modern-day Cowboy

Slumped in her chair, Lizzy dozed off and on, waking every time an aide entered to take Leonard's vitals. One of them finally noticed her injuries.

"What happened to you? Those look painful."

"Not as bad as him." Lizzy nodded toward the bed.

"Sometimes the little ones hurt the worst. Let me get you stitched up while you're here."

So, Lizzy was getting disinfected, stitched, and bandaged when Jason entered the room, followed by a mustached man in western attire.

She glanced at the cowboy, but her eyes lingered on Jason's curly red hair and bright green eyes, certain she had never been so glad to see anyone. *Except maybe Holly at the lake.*

"What happened?" he asked.

"Let's wait until I'm done getting patched up." She winked.

After the aide left, Lizzy stood and closed the door. "There's something weird going on around here." She retook her seat. "Someone tried to run me over. He pushed me out of the way." She nodded at Leonard.

"I'll want you to start at the beginning, but first, this is Ranger Borrego."

"Thank you for coming. I'm Lizzy." She shook his broad weathered hand. His presence was calming, somehow assuring everyone around him that justice would prevail.

She began her story with finding Sal at the lake, then told them everything that had happened up until the ambulance transported Leonard to the hospital.

She also sent them photos in a group text, from the crime scene and the ones Helene had given her. The ranger took notes, writing down the date and time of each incident and the names of potential suspects, even if Lizzy had dismissed them.

"Leonard claimed he didn't know who the driver was, but he was anxious enough that he asked me to stay with him here."

"I have a second ranger arriving shortly. When she gets here, you two can take a break."

A short knock on the door preceded Officer Garcia, who entered with a smile. "Leonard, bro, how're you doing?" He stared at the inert form in the bed; then glanced around.

"Lizzy? What are you doing here? Who are these guys?"

Jason, still in his uniform, stepped forward, his hand outstretched. "Captain Jason Schneider of the Harperstown police department."

"I should have known," Garcia mumbled.

"And Ranger Nelson Borrego," Jason added.

"Who invited *you* here?"

"He's here at my request. I have enough evidence to merit his involvement."

"The first thing we'll do is take a trip to the station," Borrego said. "You can get me caught up."

Garcia glowered at Lizzy, and she was thankful Jason was there.

When the door closed behind them, she walked into his embrace. Quivering, she felt herself begin to relax for the first time since she and Holly had found Sal's body.

Jason smoothed her hair and held her close. "You could have died this afternoon."

"He saved me," She nodded.

"Where's Mavis?"

"She's with one of the neighbors. The owner of the Jeep."

"Are you sure…"

"Yes. She was there with us when it drove by."

"I'm glad you called me. We'll get to the bottom of this."

"I think Leonard knows something. Otherwise, why would he be so nervous?"

"I'll get the second ranger caught up when she arrives, then let's go out to supper."

"Did you get a car?"

"I did. Pretty exciting, huh?"

"For sure. We've been stuck at that campground for almost a week."

"Do you have enough room for me to stay with you?"

Lizzy laughed. She laughed so hard she got a cramp. "Enough room," she sputtered. "Wait until you see it." She knew it was inappropriate. She knew she was just releasing pent up stress, but she couldn't help it. She laughed some more, finally pulling herself together and wiping her eyes when someone knocked.

"Hello." A middle-aged woman wearing boots and a hat like her partner poked her head around the door. "I'm Ranger Salsbury. I believe I'm expected."

"Yes. Come in," Jason said. He introduced himself and explained the situation.

"I've been in contact with Ranger Borrego. He said he'll meet with you when he's done at the station, then spell me here."

"Sounds good. Thank you."

On their way out of the hospital, Lizzy noticed her surroundings for the first time. The building was small, more like a clinic, but the halls were open and bright, the lobby clean and comfortably furnished. "It looks new, doesn't it?"

"I guess. I wasn't paying attention."

"Helene said she's the President of the Board."

"Helene?"

"The lady who gave us the victim's photographs. Where do you want to eat?"

They stopped at the reception desk and asked for a recommendation, then ended up at a restaurant advertising barbeque.

A rack of menus stood next to a sign that read, *Please seat yourselves*; so, Jason grabbed two menus and scanned the sparsely populated dining room. "Any preference?"

"No, just not near the restrooms." Lizzy chuckled.

The picnic-style tables and benches weren't designed for comfort, but the ones along the windows were smaller, as opposed to the long tables that ran through the center of the establishment.

They sat at a window overlooking the parking lot and studied the simple menu, which consisted of meats and sides in varying sizes.

"How hungry are you?" Jason asked.

"Starved. You?"

"They have a food challenge here. I don't want to race through my meal, but it seems to have everything."

"We can always take leftovers home."

"Home." He smirked. "Have you been there that long?"

"Feels like it."

Jason ordered the *Whoppin' Big Barbeque Challenge*, and they were told if they could finish it in two hours it was free.

"She shouldn't have said that. It's hard not rising to a challenge," Lizzy said.

"Just remember that if you get full, you don't have to keep eating."

Lizzy's stomach growled. "I bet Mavis is hungry too. We haven't eaten since this morning." She frowned.

The platter arrived and Lizzy gaped. "Wow."

Turkey, pastrami, fatty brisket, burnt ends, pork and beef ribs, green beans, mashed potatoes, mac and cheese, coleslaw, and garlic toast. The platter covered most of the table.

"This is a lot of food," Jason said.

"I might be drooling a little."

"Can I get you folks anything else?"

"Water?"

"Me too," Jason said.

"You got it. Startin' the timer now, just in case." She grinned.

The scattered diners whispered and craned their necks to see who was attempting the infamous challenge, as Lizzy's fork hovered indecisively over the tray.

"I don't know where to start," she said.

"If I thought we couldn't finish, I'd say start with whatever looks best."

"But we probably will so… turkey." She stabbed a piece and took a bite. "This is pretty good for turkey. Could you pass that barbeque sauce over here?"

The restaurant gradually filled as the dinner hour approached, loud voices competing with upbeat country music. Jason wanted to talk about the case, but Lizzy urged caution.

"Let's wait until we're alone. We don't know anyone here or who might repeat what."

Several diners stopped by their table and commented on the platter. "Them competitive eaters usually come with their cameras for that one. They say it's bigger than it looks."

"I might be getting a little full," Lizzy said.

"A little?" Jason wiped his fingers and surveyed the remains. "I don't think we could finish this even with Holly and Barker's help.

"Yeah. We didn't do very well. We have enough left for three more days."

"At least."

"Can we go check on Mavis now? She's been through a lot lately."

Sitting alone in her cell, Holly was surprised by a visit from a man with an impressive salt and pepper mustache and a cowboy hat.

He was tall and solid, with light blue eyes that seemed to glow.

"Ms. Schneider, my name is Ranger Borrego. Your brother asked me to help with the murder investigation."

Heart thumping, Holly sat straighter. "Is he here?"

"He is. How are they treating you?"

"Okay I guess."

"Have you eaten?"

"No. What time is it?"

He glanced at his watch. "It's five. You were arrested yesterday morning. They haven't given you anything to eat since then?"

"No. I haven't seen anyone since I got here."

He shook his head. "I'll get you something. Any requests?"

"Just a sandwich would be fine. Something I can pick at."

"Do you know why you were arrested?"

"Not exactly. It doesn't make sense. They have a bunch of pictures the victim took of me because he thought I was someone else. Why would I care about that? And I was hiking with my friend at the time of death, so I couldn't have killed him."

He studied her. "Would you mind staying here until tomorrow?"

What a strange question. "You mean you could get me out now if I really wanted you to?"

He glanced over his shoulder. "I could, but it would help me with my investigation if you'd stay."

She thought for a moment, then nodded. "Where's Jason?"

"He'll come visit tomorrow. What else can I get you, besides dinner? Water? Snacks?"

"Sure. Water especially, and maybe a book?"

"Thank you. I'll see what I can do." He turned and left, the heels of his boots clacking on the tile flooring.

Holly remained where she was, thinking about his words. She wasn't thrilled about her predicament, but at least the uncertainty was gone. Jason had come and she had allies.

When Ranger Borrego returned with food and a bag of goodies, she smiled and thanked him, feeling a twinge of hunger.

The sandwich, a triple-decker club with tater tots on the side, was accompanied by a whole pickle and a slice of homemade apple pie. Holly ate the pickle first, testing her appetite. Yesterday's breakfast seemed like a long time ago and once she had eaten the pickle, she realized how hungry she was.

She ate a quarter of the sandwich, then another before setting it aside and peeking in the goody bag. Two liter-sized bottles of water, beef jerky, cookies, chips, and a used Louis L'Amour paperback entitled *Comstock Lode*. The blurb on the back sounded mildly interesting and the book was fat; it would take her a while. *Good.* Night loomed and she doubted she would sleep.

Chapter 19

Assault

The compact white Kia Jason had rented was not quite roomy enough to accommodate his long legs. Lizzy watched as he folded himself around the steering wheel.

"Why didn't you get a bigger car?"

"The bigger ones were straying into luxury territory, and I wasn't sure how long I'd be staying." He got settled and started the car. "Do you know how to get back?"

"No. I'll pull it up on the GPS." She did so and gave him directions, noting the *Closed* sign at the entrance.

He pulled into their site and stared at the behemoth motor home.

"Enough room, you asked?"

"Why on earth did you get such a gigantic one? Isn't it hard to drive?"

"Thirty-eight feet didn't really mean anything to me, but it's comfortable. I'll give you a little tour, then we should go get Mavis."

The lock on the side door was broken and inside, chaos. Someone had done a thorough search and hadn't been neat about it.

Lizzy's heart sank. "Candy? Where are you, baby?"

The kitten's small meow came from the loft, where she sat huddled in the farthest corner.

"Come here, sweetheart. Did someone scare you?"

"Can you tell if anything's missing?" Jason asked, wandering the length of the motor home.

"No. I'll have to check, but we don't really have any valuables, other than the RV itself. And my laptop." She ran to her bedroom and checked under her pillow, letting out a deep sigh. "It's still here."

"Do you have a backup if anything happens to it?"

"Yes. At home. But still…"

"I know."

"Let's go get Mavis." Lizzy put Candy's harness on her and placed her on her shoulder. "We'll have to fix the lock. Maybe Ranger Borrego could pick one up for us."

"I'll text him and ask."

On the way to the fifth wheel, Lizzy pointed out where the hit and run occurred. She could hear Mavis barking from a distance and felt sorry for Darla.

She knocked on the door. No answer. "Something's wrong."

"Maybe she can't hear us over the barking."

"Darla?" Lizzy called. "We're here."

Inside, Mavis whined.

Pounding on the door, Lizzy called more loudly. "Darla!" She twisted the knob, and it turned. Unlocked. Glancing at Jason, she gave the door a push and stepped inside.

Mavis sprinted past her and squatted in the gravel, then ran back and barked at Lizzy.

"Where is she, girl?"

The little dog led her into the kitchen and whined again. She sat next to Darla's prone body and licked her face. *No death howl*, Lizzy thought gratefully, as Jason crouched next to Darla and felt for a pulse.

"Call for an ambulance," he said.

He took out his phone. "Schneider here. We've got an incident at the campground." As he spoke, he walked outside, leaving Lizzy and Mavis in the kitchen.

She sat with the little dog, who sniffed Candy, then climbed into Lizzy's lap. "Poor girl. You must be starving."

Based on the ingredients on the counter, Darla had been cooking when she was surprised by her attacker.

Lizzy rubbed Mavis' ears. "Sometimes I wish you could talk. You could tell us who did this."

The sirens grew louder, drowning out the sound of tires on crunching gravel. In the oppressive heat of the fifth wheel, Lizzy's tank top stuck to her torso. Sweat trickled down her back. Mavis panted with her tongue out, her fine fur sticking to Lizzy's legs. A fly buzzed.

Holding Mavis and Candy, Lizzy rose in one fluid motion and backed out of the way to make room for the first responders and Ranger Borrego.

"Has anything been touched?"

"Not since we arrived, but Mavis was inside when we got here."

"The dog?"

Lizzy nodded.

"Could you wait outside with Jason? Tight quarters."

"Yes. Can I take the pets back to the RV?"

"That's fine. I'll be over when we're done here."

Outside, the breeze revived her. She looked around for Jason, but he had disappeared. *Odd. Where'd he go?* As she passed by the party site, Frieda ran out to the road to intercept her.

"Have you seen Leonard?" she asked, slightly out of breath.

"He's in the hospital."

"Why?"

"He got hit by a car. He's okay, but he has a broken leg."

Her face crumpled. "What do I do now? What happened at Darla's?"

"How do you know Darla?"

"She's my stepmom," Freida mumbled. "Six years older than me." She made a face.

"She's being taken to the hospital too."

"What happened to her? What's even going on? I feel like the last man standing after the zombie apocalypse." Her eyes widened and her voice rose with her anxiety.

"You should probably go to the hospital and see them."

"Yeah. Thanks."

Lizzy watched her shuffle back toward the campfire, head down and shoulders hunched. She didn't see a car and wondered if Frieda had transportation. *Should I ask? Where's Jim? Is she alone out here?*

She continued her walk back to site forty-eight, feeling Mavis' weight, and when she arrived she found Jason, working on the door.

"I was wondering where you went."

"I wasn't needed for the moment. I hope this is okay."

"It's great." Lizzy grinned. "I need to feed these rascals before they try to eat each other."

"We can't have that." He stood and backed out of her way.

"Thanks for fixing the lock."

Mavis and Candy raced around in circles, the kitchen sounding like feeding time at the zoo.

"Good grief. Settle down."

Mavis didn't wait for her obligatory doggy massage. She inhaled her food like the canine vacuum she was.

Lizzy wandered back outside and handed Jason a beer. "Want me to make a fire?"

"I can do that," he said, accepting the beer.

"I want to show off my new skills."

"All right. Let's see what you've got."

They didn't have long to wait before Ranger Borrego arrived. He declined Lizzy's offer of beer. "I'm still on duty but thank you." He sat on a log by the fire and crossed his arms. "Our suspects are dropping like flies."

"How's Holly doing?"

"They put her in a cell and haven't interacted with her at all. I got her some dinner and a book to help pass the time."

"You couldn't get her released?" Lizzy asked.

Borrego stared at his boots. "I could; if I wanted to."

She looked at him sharply.

"I asked her if she would stay a little longer. I don't want to tip our hand too soon. You two can visit her tomorrow while I continue investigating."

"Do you have any idea what happened to Darla?"

"Someone hit her on the head, hard enough to kill her. I found a bloody rolling pin under the table. A single blonde hair. Prints everywhere, multiple people, but none on the rolling pin. You said the front door was closed but not locked. Is that correct?"

"Yes."

"She probably let them in. They were known to her. Hopefully she'll gain consciousness and be able to tell us who."

"I imagine it was the same person who broke into the RV," Jason said.

"Very likely. Stick together while you're out here. Our murderer seems to be getting bolder."

Lizzy shivered.

A police cruiser screeched to a halt behind Jason's Kia.

Chief Elkhurst got out and stomped toward the campfire with his shoulders hunched and his hands fisted. "Why wasn't I notified? I need to know what's going on. First Salamander. Now Darla. Is someone targeting me? Who's next? Me? My wife?"

One of Ranger Borrego's eyebrows rose. "That's an interesting take on it. Someone was certainly trying to frame you for your son's murder."

"The girl couldn't have done it. She's locked up." He narrowed his eyes at Lizzy. "You." He took a step forward.

"Don't even think about it," Jason warned in a low voice.

"Who are you?"

"This is your prisoner's brother, Captain Schneider," Borrego said. "You might want to stop trying to pin all this on strangers and look a little closer to home."

"And you might want to mind your own business. We don't need no stinking rangers butting in."

Borrego gazed at him in silence.

The chief spun around and stomped back to his cruiser, then drove off, his tires spewing gravel.

"What would he have done if you weren't here?" Lizzy asked. "He's kind of scary."

"He was looking for me. I doubt he'll be back."

"I've been thinking." Both men looked at Lizzy.

"Before we found Sal's body, Holly and I saw Jim leaving the area. I don't think he saw us. He hasn't been around lately. Garcia said he was arrested for trying to break in. Now there's been another break in. Maybe you could locate him and ask him about the time of Sal's murder?'

Borrego made a note.

"Also, I don't know if it's important, but I found out that Darla Gross is Frieda's stepmother."

"Who's Frieda?" Jason asked.

"She's Jim's girlfriend, the one who invited us to the party. And her father is the high school football coach."

"All of this apparently means something to you," Borrego said.

"They were all at the party. Jim had two football players with him when he tried to break in. He was at or near the scene of the crime when Sal was murdered. Coach Gross supposedly doesn't know where Darla's been staying, but he was at the underage party with his daughter, just down the road. It all seems overly coincidental, doesn't it?"

"We'll track them down tomorrow." Borrego stood and took several folded papers out of his back pocket. "These are copies I made of work logs for the times in question. I have to go spell Ranger Salsbury but take a look at them and I'll be in touch." He tipped his hat and turned, then sauntered toward his vehicle, still parked in front of the fifth wheel.

Lizzy smiled at the image his departing figure evoked, that of a stoic lawman from the old west and a plot idea began to blossom.

Chapter 20

Conference at the Station

When Jason awoke, he was disoriented. Laying on his side, with his legs half on, half off the sofa, his lower body felt anchored in place. Mavis licked his face. He craned his neck to see Lizzy lying on his hip and remembered. He hadn't wanted to disturb her when she fell asleep and leaned against him. He supposed he must have fallen asleep too and tipped over.

Mavis barked, impatient, and Lizzy opened her eyes. She jerked upright and blinked. "Sorry, I'll take her out."

"I can do it. I didn't want to wake you."

"I'll make coffee then."

Grateful for the brisk air and a moment of solitude, he watched Mavis search for the perfect spot and thought about his relationship with Lizzy. In some ways she was like a sister. They got along well, despite their occasional squabbles. But there was something else, bubbling beneath the surface. He knew she fought it, and he told himself he was relieved. Her standoffishness meant he didn't have to make a conscious choice. He could just enjoy her company. *I have to be more careful.* His biggest fear was losing her friendship and mistakes like that morning endangered their status quo.

By the time Mavis was ready to go inside for breakfast, Jason had his emotions under control. He entered breezily behind her and accepted a cup of coffee.

Lizzy, her hair sprouting in every direction, stood with the refrigerator door open. "We have lots of leftovers, unless you want me to make something."

"Leftovers are fine. What've we got?"

"Quiche, pizza, and barbeque."

"Quiche sounds good."

"Warm or cold?"

"Cold."

"I tried both yesterday and I like cold better too." She placed the quiche, plates, forks, and Tapatio on the table then sat across from him. "I'm sorry for falling asleep on you."

"If it had been Barker, it would have been weird." He grinned, making light of it. Barker, his sergeant, was dating Holly.

Lizzy laughed.

"He wanted to come, but we couldn't both leave."

"Plus, he's supposed to meet up with us in LA." Pausing, Lizzy said, "I think Holly wants to go home. She said so the other day. I don't know if I can do this on my own."

Looking into her eyes, Jason saw the fear, the uncertainty. "I understand." He wanted to volunteer to take Holly's place, but the thought of that much proximity made him nervous. He decided to think about it before he said anything.

"How's your timeline?" he asked.

"If we don't leave in a day or two we won't make it."

"Do you have any idea who's behind all this?"

"Yes, but I don't understand why, and I don't have the resources to check people's alibis."

"Why don't we start with the logs Borrego gave us last night? I was too tired to examine them very closely." He spread out the papers. "The first one shows why they released the chief. He was in a meeting with his superior. A solid alibi unless the superintendent lied for him."

"Okay. None of the others have much of an alibi though. Officer Mills was running a speed trap, Garcia was on lunch, and Quirk was doing paperwork. Mills is the policewoman?"

"No idea. The only ones I've met so far are Garcia and the chief."

"How about when I was at the lake?"

"Mills was at the station, the chief was off, and Garcia and Quirk were out looking for you."

"Not very helpful. Garcia said the chief might have been out searching for his missing button."

"You said you looked carefully at the person's silhouette to try to figure out who it was, right?"

"Have you ever tried to do that? With nothing nearby to gauge size, it's nearly impossible."

"Okay, well, during the time of the hit and run, Mills and the chief were at the station, Garcia was off, and Quirk was patrolling."

"And yesterday?"

"Mills and the chief were off, Quirk was on dinner break, and Garcia was patrolling."

Lizzy sighed.

"With any luck, we'll be able to get Holly released today. I'll text Borrego and see if he can arrange a visit." He looked down. "Where'd the quiche go?"

"You ate it."

"Not by myself I didn't."

"I might have helped a little. We can have barbeque for lunch."

When Lizzy and Jason entered the station, they were met with icy stares. Ranger Borrego glanced at the local officers as he walked past them to greet the visitors.

"Welcome. I've arranged a visit for you, Lizzy, and the rest of us will have an impromptu meeting. I'd like you to join us, Captain."

Lizzy was worried about Holly and hoping she would be able to leave with them. She remembered her brief incarceration in Harperstown and wouldn't wish it on anyone. *At least Borrego gave her a choice and got her a book.* She followed him down a dimly lit hall to the cell at the end, where Holly sat, her back against the wall, reading a thick battered paperback.

She looked up when she heard the ranger's boots and smiled. "Lizzy! You came."

"Of course I did, as soon as I was allowed."

Borrego opened the cell door and turned to leave. "Enjoy your visit. We'll discuss your predicament and then you'll be free to go."

Ranger Borrego strode into the meeting room and observed the five officers seated around the rectangular table. "As you all know," he said, "I am here at the request of Captain Schneider, whose sister Holly was arrested for the murder of Salamander Elkhurst. We are all aware, I believe, that Holly did not kill Salamander. She didn't know him, the photos he took were a matter of mistaken identity, and she was hiking with her friend at the time of death. We still have a case to solve, but we have plenty of suspects without trying to pin it on a convenient outsider."

He continued. "Additionally, while she has been incarcerated, we've had two more attempted murders at the campground. Logically speaking, those attempts were made by the same person. Therefore, I would like to recommend you release Holly at once and interview each of our suspects to find out where they were yesterday afternoon."

"And if we don't?" the chief asked.

"Then we will have a conversation with the superintendent."

Chief Elkhurst frowned. "You heard the man. Release Ms. Schneider then get on those interviews."

A great clatter arose as everyone pushed their wooden chairs back and stood. "Ranger Borrego, could you stay? I'd like a word."

Borrego signaled Jason to remain before turning to face the chief.

"Are you thinking we've got a dirty cop on our hands?"

"Not necessarily, but we're certainly dealing with a local."

Elbows on the table and fingers steepled, the chief rested his chin lightly on his fingertips and looked at the ranger. "Someone, possibly the murderer and possibly a cop, framed me so well I might have arrested myself. They had to release me because I had an indisputable alibi. I was in a meeting with the superintendent until the call came in."

Borrego nodded.

"We're looking for someone who was able to commandeer my uniform shirt and return it; someone who might appear to have an alibi but really doesn't."

"I believe your son's motorcycle and camera are missing as well."

"Yes."

"Has anyone searched his room?"

"I was going to, but I just can't."

"Would you like Captain Schneider and me to take care of that?"

"Yes. I'll give you the address and let my wife know. When will you be going?" He scribbled the address on a sticky note.

"We'll head over now. Pay close attention to the alibis for all four incidents so we can start narrowing down our list of suspects."

"Four?"

Borrego glanced at Jason, who jerked his head slightly to the right, not a shake exactly, just a cautionary signal. "Three, I guess." He stood and took the sticky note. "We'll be back after the search and compare results."

They shook hands before Jason and the ranger left the conference room.

On the way to the Elkhurst home, Borrego asked, "Why didn't you want me to tell the chief about the *seeker*, as Lizzy calls him?"

"At the moment, the only people who know about that incident are Lizzy and the person who was there with her.

135

"Eventually we'll have to check alibis for that time, but…"

"I see. Yes. It might be advantageous to have one incident under our hats." He pulled up in front of the chief's house and Jason noticed an old woman and her dog looking out of the front window next door.

Mrs. Elkhurst opened the door before they knocked. "Come in. I've been expecting you. Sal's room is upstairs, the first on the right. We haven't been in there since—"

"I understand, ma'am. Please accept our condolences. We won't be long." Borrego led the way upstairs and opened the bedroom door.

The two men stepped inside and stopped, glancing around and then at each other. The room was completely impersonal except for one wall littered with photographs. The single bed was covered with a plain white comforter. The curtains were white, and a mirror hung above a brown dresser. A computer and a stack of photography magazines rested on a brown desk.

"It's like a guest room," Jason said. "Except for that one wall."

Borrego approached the wall in question, scrutinizing the pictures. "Was he a stalker?"

"Someone told Lizzy he wanted to be a paparazzi. Is that the same girl in all of them?"

"Looks like it."

Jason studied the collage carefully as Borrego wandered toward the bathroom. The earliest shots showed the girl in elementary school, the most recent at her funeral. But as he followed Sal's documentation of her life, he discovered one that was out of sequence. It was similar to the photos Lizzy had shown him, with one difference. Not only was she at the party, she was hugging Frank Garcia.

"Borrego?"

"Yeah? What's up? You should see the dark room he made in the bathroom." He sauntered over to where Jason was standing.

"What do you suppose this means? These are pictures of her funeral."

"I guess it means she's not dead and Garcia knows about it."

"I wonder if he just found out, or if he's known for a while. And what was he doing at that party? Lizzy said it was an underage drinking party and someone was selling drugs."

The ranger let out a low whistle. "Sounds like a motive to me."

Chapter 21

Betrayal

Helene recognized a ranger when she saw one. The man with him, however, was a mystery. They arrived next door and Marjorie, clearly expecting them, ushered them inside.

"What's going on?" Mary asked from the sofa.

"Maybe Marjorie's next." Helene chuckled. "Since all their suspects have either been arrested or taken to the hospital, they must be getting desperate."

"I need to see Leonard."

"Just be patient, dear. Y'all have options right now, but as soon as you go showing your face around town, they'll be gone."

"I'm so sick of it. If I'd been in my right mind I would've told Leonard not to listen to him."

"It's gotten more complicated now. We need to talk it out with him before you do something you can't take back."

Mary looked down at her hands, twisting her wedding band round and round her finger.

I'll have to keep an eye on her so she doesn't do anything stupid. Leonard was Helene's favorite grandson, and she kept trying to help him, but he'd gotten in so deep that she didn't know how. All she knew was if one of them went down, they'd all go down.

Mary stood, her stature startling Helene as usual. "I'm going to go upstairs and lie down."

"That's a good idea. I'll get dinner on in just a bit." Helene resumed her post at the front window. *Should I give Patricia's snapshots to the ranger? Or send her to see that writer? How can I get him out of the way without hurting Leonard?*

After Jason and Borrego left the Elkhurst home, they drove to the high school to speak with Coach Gross. He stood as they entered, a hulking man whose muscles were turning to fat. Bleary eyes and a slack mouth hinted that he had been drinking that morning.

"Good afternoon. I'm Ranger Nelson Borrego and this is Captain Schneider. We'd like to ask you some questions."

"About what?"

"Let's begin with your family. Do you mind if we have a seat."

"Sure," the coach waved expansively.

Once they were all seated, Borrego continued. "I understand that you have a daughter named Frieda."

"What's she done now? Knocked over a grocery store?"

"She hasn't done anything, as far as I know. Has she been in trouble in the past?"

"It's my fault. I spoiled her. Now she won't listen, and she let that punk Jim get her pregnant."

"How old is she?"

"Twenty-five. Same as him. They were in school together. Kicked him off the team for doing drugs."

"Did you know he got two of your players to help him with an attempted break in?"

The coach thrust himself out of his chair, his face purple. "Now he's gone too far."

"Didn't the police talk to you about that?" Jason asked.

Sinking back into his chair, he said, "Maybe they did. I don't remember."

"Do you know where we can find him?"

"He lives in one of those camper vans. His mom might know. Wanda. She owns the hair salon."

Borrego slid a piece of paper toward Coach Gross. "Could you tell us where you were and what you were doing at these times?"

"No idea." He barked a short mirthless laugh. "But any time between eight and four, I'm here. And when I'm not here, I'm at the *Trough*. You can ask Art."

"Who's Art?"

"The owner."

"Thank you. That'll be all."

Their next stop was the *Trough*. Jason followed Borrego into the dimly lit bar and stood briefly, letting his eyes adjust. Country music vied with jocular voices and clinking glassware.

"Will you be having lunch?" a middle-aged waitress asked.

"Yes," Borrego said. "And could you send Art over when he has a moment?"

She showed them to a booth tucked away in the farthest corner and handed them each a one-page menu. "Can I get you something to drink while you wait?"

"Water would be great."

"I'll have iced tea," Jason said.

She hurried off without comment.

Studying the menu, Borrego said, "I figured we'll have to eat at some point. I wonder if the food is any good."

"They have a pretty robust lunch crowd," Jason said. "It can't be too bad."

Borrego just chuckled.

They both ordered burgers, which were delivered by Art himself. Of average height and build, his head reflected the overhead lights. His neat mustache and goatee took away slightly from the air of a librarian he projected.

"Your burgers, gentlemen. I'm Art. You asked to speak with me?"

"Yes, thank you. I'm Ranger Nelson Borrego and this is Captain Schneider."

He stood and shook hands. "Could you join us for a few minutes?"

Art sat with them and waited.

"We've spoken to Coach Gross, and he said that outside of work hours, he can be found here."

"Sometimes during work hours too," Art said wryly.

"Let's begin with Saturday night. Can you recall if he was here?"

"The thing is, he's here so often that I might only notice if he's not. On Saturday night, another customer said something about his daughter and some big party out at the campground. He got mad and stumbled out the door earlier than usual. I remember hoping he wasn't driving."

"How about the next day? Are you open on Sundays?"

"Yes, and he was here all afternoon. He got into a pathetic fist fight with the guy who made him mad the night before, then demanded frozen peas to use as an ice pack." Art shook his head.

"Ok. One more. Was he here yesterday?"

"Yes…he came in for dinner and stayed until closing. I remember because he and a couple of his friends were arguing about sports. It's always something."

"Thank you very much. That's all we needed to know."

"Happy to be of assistance, but I'm afraid your food has gone cold. Would you like me to have the chef heat it up for you?"

"No, that's okay. We don't want to take up any more of your time."

Art left them and Jason took a bite of his burger and nodded. "Mm. It's still good."

"It is. I bet it's great when it's fresh."

"I guess we can cross the coach off our list," Jason said after a few minutes.

"Yeah. He wasn't at the top anyway, but his presence at the party and the assault on his wife made me curious."

Jason left his keys with Lizzy, so once Holly was released, they returned to the motor home. Mavis sounded the alarm before they got to the door. She wagged her tail so enthusiastically Lizzy thought she might strain something. Holly ran inside, calling Candy, who meowed and rubbed against her leg. Snuggling the kitten close, Holly sat with her and said, "I'm sorry I left you alone. I heard you had a little scare." Candy purred.

"Was it a terrible mess?" Holly asked.

"It looked worse than it was. I never did figure out what they were searching for."

"The photos?"

"But we already gave them to the police."

"We know that, but maybe whoever broke in didn't."

"I suppose. But then they tried to kill Darla. What does she have to do with any of it?"

Holly tilted her head. "They tried to run you over with her car, right? Maybe she knows more than she let on."

"I'd hate to think so." She stared off into space for a few minutes, reenacting the scene in her mind, then shook her head and stood. "Hey. Let's go swimming."

"Aren't they back from the hospital now?"

"Who knows. But what are they going to do, have us arrested?" Lizzy laughed. "Come on. It's been a brutal week, and we need a little fun."

"I'm onboard, as long as we can take Candy."

"The more the merrier. Maybe we should teach her to swim."

They got changed and Lizzy texted Jason to let him know where they'd be. With Leonard and Darla in the hospital, and the other campers gradually allowed to leave, the campground was quiet and empty. Their footsteps on the gravel road and Mavis' intermittent barking were the only sounds interrupting nature's tranquil symphony.

They turned a second corner and were approaching the pool when laughter rang out. Lizzy grasped Holly's arm and whispered, "Wait here." She handed her Mavis' leash and tiptoed forward. She needn't have worried about them hearing her footsteps. Music played from a Bluetooth speaker as they laughed and hollered, splashing and dunking each other in the water. Lizzy froze. Only their swimsuits were missing. Not wanting to make things more awkward, she began quietly backing away, but Mavis had other ideas. Recognizing Garcia's voice, perhaps, she chose that moment to begin barking. She yanked her leash from Holly's grasp and raced past Lizzy to the fence.

Lizzy cringed and followed. "Hi," she greeted the swimmers with a small wave. "Sorry to intrude."

"We'll be leaving soon," Mary said, "but we don't even have towels."

"Don't worry. We'll just come back later."

"Thanks. We didn't plan on swimming but got to daring each other, and… you know how it is with cousins." She grinned.

Lizzy produced a half smile and moved away.

"Well, that was awkward," she said to Holly after she and Mavis had rejoined her.

"They're *cousins?* Eww. Sorry about Mavis. She caught me off guard."

"I don't know about you, but I've kind of lost interest in the pool. Wanna just go back to the campsite?"

Chapter 22

Darla's Statement

After lunch, Jason and Ranger Borrego drove to the hospital to check in with Salsbury. "Mrs. Gross is awake," she reported.

"Good," Borrego said. "Why don't you take a break? We'll hold down the fort."

"Thanks. I could use something to eat."

To Jason he said, "We've got them in the same room so one of us can guard both. They don't seem to mind."

The center dividing curtain was pulled back and the television was on. Darla and Leonard were laughing as they played along with Family Feud. "Take a nap," she yelled. "Eat vegetables," Leonard shouted.

"Don't you two get reprimanded for making so much noise?"

"Nah. They moved everyone away from us hooligans." Leonard snorted. "Who are you?"

"My apologies. I'm Ranger Nelson Borrego and this is Captain Schneider, here on behalf of his sister Holly." He lifted his hat.

"Holly of the giant RV?" Darla asked.

"Yes, ma'am. He and Lizzy found you yesterday."

"I was wondering how I got here. No one seemed to know."

"Do you remember who struck you?"

"Ye-es… but I think I might be mixed up because it doesn't seem very probable."

"Why don't you tell us who you think it was, and we can discuss it. Your mind might be able to unravel what happened if you talk it through."

"Well, I remember taking out ingredients to make something both Mavis and I could eat.

"She was making a terrible commotion. Then I went to answer the door, and Marjorie Elkhurst was standing there. I was surprised because we had never spoken. I didn't think she even knew about the fifth wheel." Her face puckered up before her hand went to the bandage on her head. "Augh. That hurts."

"The doctor said you got hit hard enough to kill you. We found the rolling pin under the table."

"The rolling pin?"

"We'll get to that. You opened the door?"

"Yes. She seemed agitated."

"What made you think that?"

"I… she…" Darla's eyes rolled up to the left. "She was shifting her weight from one leg to the other and glancing around. Her breathing was kind of noisy. Fidgety. That's it. Anyway, she asked if she could come in and if I couldn't make the dog be quiet, and I told her Mavis was hungry. I explained that the sooner I got her fed, the sooner she'd settle down, so I went back to making dinner. Marjorie paced around, looking at things and asking questions. Mavis stood at my feet, glancing up at me and barking at her."

"Was she wagging her tail and just making noise? Or did she seem like she was in aggressive guard-dog mode?" Jason asked.

"I'm no expert, but it seemed to me like she wanted Marjorie to leave. Maybe she just wanted her dinner. I don't know."

"What happened next?" Borrego asked.

"Well, she started asking me about her husband, how well I knew him, how often he came over. Her voice got higher and angrier. Then she brought up Sal. She accused me of murder, and I dropped the pan."

"What happened after that?"

"I don't know. I woke up here."

"What was in the pan?"

"I was sautéing vegetables and about to add ground beef. It must have made a terrible mess. Mavis didn't get burned?"

"I don't think so. What was Marjorie wearing?" Jason asked.

"I don't… wait, I remember. It was some kind of frilly white blouse with long sleeves. It looked very light weight. And bright pink slacks."

"Shoes?"

"I didn't notice. Is that important?"

"Maybe not. You said you weren't sure if it was Marjorie who put you in the hospital. Do you have any other ideas?"

"Not really. I didn't know how I got here. But you said you and Lizzy found me and called an ambulance?"

Jason nodded and glanced at Leonard, who was listening with rapt attention.

"The last thing I remember is Marjorie accusing me of murdering Sal. But why would she hit me and leave? Did she mean to kill me? Or she just lashed out and ran away? The whole thing seems like one of those strange dreams that don't make sense when you wake up."

"Yes, I understand," Borrego said. "Have you seen your stepdaughter lately?"

"Frieda? Does she have something to do with this?"

"Not that I know of. Do the two of you get along?"

"It's complicated. I'm not much older than her so she doesn't refer to me as her stepmother. She doesn't like it that I'm married to her dad." She tilted her head. "But we're allies. We both know how John is when he's drinking, and we keep each other's secrets. Complicated."

"Thank you very much for your assistance. I think that's all for now."

"Could you ask Lizzy to come talk to me?" Leonard asked from his bed. "It's important."

"Is it something that could further our investigation?"

"No, I just need some advice."

"I'll bring her by later," Borrego assured him.

On their way out of the hospital, he said, "Darla has wounds on both sides of her head. The doctor thinks she was struck from behind with the rolling pin and hit the right side of her head on the counter when she fell. I found a single blonde hair, which is likely Marjorie Elkhurst's."

"If there was a mess from the falling pan, someone cleaned it up," Jason said. "But they didn't take the rolling pin. Do you think there might have been a third person?"

"Only one way to find out."

Chapter 23

Leonard's Story

When Ranger Borrego parked behind a police cruiser at the swimming pool, Jason immediately thought the worst. His pulse quickened as he threw the car door open and sprinted to the fence, then skidded to a halt, taking in the scene. Borrego was right behind him.

Water sloshed as Garcia and his date enjoyed an intimate interlude. His back was to the gate and the woman, leaning against the side of the pool, had her head back and her eyes closed.

Jason hadn't met her, but he recognized her from Sal's photo shrine. He took out his phone and began to record. According to the police log, Garcia was scheduled for patrol. Jason opened the gate and strolled to a small round table where he and Borrego sat on plastic chairs.

The woman opened her eyes and gasped.

"No. Not yet," Garcia murmured.

She pounded on his shoulder and tried to push him away. "We have company."

He turned and froze. "What are you doing here?" he demanded. "Have some decency. This isn't a spectator sport."

"Good one. Decency. That's a public pool," Borrego said. "And you're on duty. Guess what that means."

"What?"

"That means you have no alibi for the time of Salamander's death."

Garcia stared at him for a moment before his eyes narrowed. "Now just a minute. Just because I'm taking a break doesn't mean I don't do my job."

He looked at Jason. "Are you recording this? Put your phone away."

"Turn around, Mary," he said, before hoisting himself out of the pool and stomping toward Jason with his fists clenched. Borrego stood and Garcia swung at him; his attention still focused on Jason. The ranger ducked out of the way and sent a straight punch into Garcia's solar plexus. He crumpled, gasping for breath. Jason returned his phone to his pocket.

"We'll be going now," Borrego said. "If I see you here when I get back, I'll arrest both of you on the spot."

<hr>

The hammock swung gently between two trees. Lizzy lay in the partial sun, her leg thrown over one side. She heard the car, but didn't move; not wanting to let go of the peaceful dream-like state she floated in. Mavis barked and she could picture the little dog wagging her tail.

"Lizzy? You said you'd be at the pool."

"It was occupied."

"We saw. Where's Holly?"

"She's taking her post-incarceration shower." Lizzy opened her eyes and smiled up at Jason.

"Leonard wants to talk to you. I don't want Holly to be here by herself, so Ranger Borrego's going to give you a ride, if that's okay."

"Yeah, that's fine. I was so comfortable." She rolled off the hammock and onto her feet. "I wonder what Leonard wants."

"I'll verify some details while we're in town then we should regroup," Borrego said.

"Holly's got a casserole in the oven. Why don't you join us for dinner?"

Not a talkative man, Borrego drove Lizzy to the hospital in silence. He dropped her off and said he'd be back within the hour.

Upstairs, her knock was answered by Ranger Salsbury, who left to take a break. Leonard looked toward her when she entered. Darla had been discharged, so the two of them were alone.

"I'm glad you came," he said. "I need some advice."

Recalling Mary and Garcia in the pool, she wondered whether she should tell him. She drug a chair to the side of his bed and sat.

"I'll have to start at the beginning. It's a long story."

"That's okay. I have time."

"Well, Mary and I got hitched ten years ago. She was eighteen and I was twenty. We were poor, but so in love it didn't matter. On our first anniversary, we decided to take out five-million-dollar life insurance policies on each other as our gifts. That way, if anything happened to one of us, the other could at least be comfortable."

"Whose idea was that? Yours?"

"It was Mary's idea, but I agreed with her."

Lizzy nodded slowly.

"Several years ago, we were out at the lake with friends. We were in a rowboat, the two of us, and she was scaring me. I can't swim. I was wearing a life jacket, but the water always makes me nervous. She was standing with one foot on each side and rocking the boat back and forth, laughing. The more I told her to stop, the harder she rocked the boat, until it flipped over. I was stuck underneath and completely panicked, even now I remember that feeling, the boat pressing down and I couldn't duck under it because of the life jacket."

Leonard's chest visibly rose and fell. He gripped his sheet.

"By the time I got out from under the boat, Mary had disappeared. I looked around, tried to see under the water but it was too murky. I called to some friends in another boat, and they helped me search but we couldn't find her. The police dragged the lake, searched the shoreline, no sign of her. After about six months, she was declared dead and the life insurance company paid out the five million."

Leonard looked into Lizzy's eyes with a pained expression. "I didn't care about the money. I didn't care about anything. I wished it had been me instead of her."

How would it feel to love someone that much? "What did you do? How did you carry on?"

"At first, I just worked on my cabin. I didn't go anywhere, didn't talk to anyone. I worked so hard I collapsed into sleep each night. I didn't shave or cut my hair; I didn't even shower. Then one day my cousin came to see me. He said he found Mary, but she'd lost her memory. She was staying with some farmers on the far side of the lake. He took me to see her and between the two of us, we kept visiting until she started to remember. One day she asked if I would take her home."

"You must have been very happy."

"At first I was, but she was different. And we had the life insurance thing hanging over our heads. Frank said she had to stay hidden because if they found out, I'd go to jail and lose her again. But Mary didn't like the isolation. She wanted to see her friends and family. Frank visited her sometimes, but she was restless."

"I don't think you would've gone to jail if you'd notified them right away. It was just a mistake." Lizzy canted her head. "You said you hadn't spent the money, right?"

Leonard, his leg raised in a heavy cast, shifted, trying to make himself more comfortable in the narrow hospital bed. "I spent a lot when she came home, on clothes and furniture, but nothing made her happy. Then my cousin decided to take advantage of the situation. He came to me with a proposition. I host the campground parties and sell the kids what he called *party favors.*"

"Drugs?"

He couldn't meet her eyes. "Yeah. I don't know where he gets them. He expects me to sell whatever he sends my way, and I get a small cut. But Lizzy," he looked up then. "I don't want to sell drugs and things are getting out of hand.

"I don't know if everything's connected, but I have a bad feeling and I want out. I don't know what to do. I need help."

"Who all knows about Mary?"

"Just family…oh, and Darla. Sally came by the site and tried to blackmail me. Little weasel. She saw his photos."

Not to mention Holly, Jason, Borrego and me. "Does Freida have any personal interest in this?"

"No, she's one of Mary's cousins and she happened to see her at the party."

"Why was Mary there? Wasn't that risky?"

"It was, but she's a strong-minded woman and she decided she was going. Leave it to Sally to pick that night."

"Where were you the day he was murdered?"

"I didn't kill him," Leonard said quickly. "I have enough problems without adding a murder charge. I was at the campsite with Mary, sleeping it off."

"I believe you. Let me give it some thought." She stood. "I'll be back to see you tomorrow or the day after."

"There's one more thing. If you want proof, I have it at home. Mary's staying with Gran, so the house is empty. The front door has a code lock and the alarm number's the same, 4-8-3-5. There's a journal in the top drawer of my desk that has the dates, type of drugs, buyers, amounts. It's all there."

"Does Mary know about this?" *I can't tell him about her. It'll crush him.*

"No, only Gran. I never told Mary about the drugs."

Chapter 24

Unexpected Witnesses

anger Borrego was leaning against the hallway wall with his arms crossed and his hat down over his eyes when Lizzy exited Leonard's room. She might have thought him sleeping if he hadn't immediately stood alert at her appearance.

"Would you be willing to make one more stop before we return?"

"Sure. Where to?"

"A hair salon."

"Your hair looks okay to me." She winked.

He raised an eyebrow. "If it gets even half an inch long I get a hat head."

Lizzy snorted, thinking of her own unruly mop.

Once they parked and entered the *Masterpiece Salon*, Borrego asked for Wanda.

Wearing a tie-dyed smock, her masses of curly black hair piled on top of her head, she approached with a smile. "What can I do for you?"

"I'm Ranger Nelson Borrego. I was wondering if you could tell me where to find your son, Jim."

Her smile vanished. "Is he in trouble?"

"No, but he may have information that could help me with my investigation."

Hand on her chest, she said, "He's asked to stay with us for a couple of days while he repairs his van. I'll write down the address for you." She scribbled on a small piece of notepaper and handed it to him.

"Thank you, ma'am. I'd appreciate it if you didn't call him after we leave. I'd rather not have to look for him again."

"I understand," she whispered. "You're not going to arrest him, right?"

"That's not my intention."

Lizzy looked back as they left and said, "She's going for the phone."

Borrego frowned and she thought he might have been driving a little above the speed limit on their way to Wanda's house.

A young woman with mousey hair and large ears opened the front door when he knocked. "He told me to tell you he's not here, but he is."

"Who?"

"Jim. Mom called and said you were coming." She observed them through thick glasses. "Oh, I'm Patricia. Come in."

Upstairs, she banged on the second door on the left and yelled, "Jim, you have company." She stepped back quickly when Jim yanked the door open and threw a wild right hook. He stumbled and fell, landing on his right shoulder and looking up to find Ranger Borrego, arms crossed looking faintly amused. "If that had connected I would have to arrest you for assault. Could we have a word?"

Jim nodded and bade Borrego and Lizzy to enter. "You're not invited," he told his sister. "Traitor."

Once he had closed the door, he sat on his desk chair and motioned them to sit on the edge of the bed. "I know Lizzy and Mom said you're a ranger."

Borrego introduced himself. "I'd like you to tell me about the party. About Freida and her father."

"Oh. That's easy. Her dad is such a jerk."

"He cut you from the football team for taking drugs."

"Yeah, except I wasn't taking drugs. He got the wrong guy, and I didn't want to snitch. I was looking at a full-ride scholarship and he ruined my life."

"So, you're getting even through his daughter?"

He grinned, a mischievous glint in his eyes, and Lizzy understood Freida's attraction. He ran his hand through curly brown hair. "I like Frieda. She stays with me sometimes, so she doesn't have to go home. At the party, he showed up bombed and I told him she was having my baby, just to goad him. He lost his mind and demanded she go home with him. When she said no, he told me to meet him at the lake the next day and he'd teach me a lesson."

"Why did you try to break into the RV?" Lizzy asked.

"I was just trying to get his players into trouble, although with a nice rig like that, I figured you might have some expensive stuff."

"We don't, actually. It's a rental. But that's beside the point. Holly and I saw you near the scene of the crime, right before we found Sal's body."

"Yeah, like I said, the coach told me to meet him there. I wasn't going to at first, but then I thought about Frieda and thought maybe someone should teach her dad a lesson." He swallowed visibly and shifted his weight.

"Did you see the body?"

He nodded, focused on Lizzy as if Borrego didn't exist. "I didn't kill him. I swear. I didn't have any reason to."

"What did you do when you saw him?"

"I just stood there for a second. I remember weird little details, like he was laying on his hand..." He shook his head. "Then I realized I'd get blamed for it, so I ran."

"Did you notice any other details?" Borrego asked.

"You believe me?"

"I believe that you were there."

"I recognized him because of his weird hair. And I noticed the water was shallow and barely moving around his head. I wondered how he ended up face down in just a couple inches of water." He swallowed, his face reflecting the memory. "I didn't really like him but seeing him like that... it was awful."

"Maybe the coach arrived early and killed him before you got there," Borrego suggested.

"I would love to believe that." Jim's brows furrowed. "I hate the man. But I don't think he could've done it. He's lazy and weak, and lately he's been drunk all the time."

"He managed to get to the party," Lizzy said.

"Pure luck if you ask me. Is Frieda okay?"

"The last time I saw her she was alone at the campsite."

"I need to go check on her. Are you going to arrest me?"

"Not at the moment but stick around."

"Thanks, man." Jim grabbed his keys and raced down the stairs. "Sorry, Sis," he hollered over his shoulder as he left.

Patricia peeked her head through a door across the hall, looking toward the staircase before taking two steps toward Lizzy and Borrego. "I—Did he…" Her face turned pink, and she adjusted her glasses. "Salamander was my best friend," she said. "Jim and his friends always bullied us. I was worried he might have…" She clenched her small hands into fists. "Did he have anything to do with Salamander's death?"

"We don't have any evidence that points to him," Borrego said. "Did he have reason to want him dead?"

"I don't think so. I just thought… I thought maybe his bullying went too far. Maybe it was an accident." Her voice quavered.

"It was no accident. Whoever killed Sal meant for him to die."

"Then it was probably about the photographs."

"How do you know about those?" Borrego asked sharply.

"He came over the night before he died and showed them to me. There weren't any of Jim."

Poor thing. It must be terrible to suffer that kind of loss and suspect family of causing it. "Are you okay? Do you have someone you can talk to?"

"I went to see Helene. She understands."

<h1 style="text-align:center">Chapter 25</h1>

<h2 style="text-align:center">Marjorie Comes Clean</h2>

Holly had the table set and dinner ready when Lizzy and Borrego returned. Jason was watching basketball with Candy, and Mavis was standing alert in the kitchen. "Anybody hungry?" Holly called as they entered.

Lizzy's stomach made ominous noises and Jason laughed. He shut off the television and joined them at the table. "How'd it go with Leonard?"

"He told me a lot of stuff. Darla's been discharged. Was she able to tell you who tried to kill her?"

"Help yourselves," Holly said, handing the serving spoon to Borrego.

He took a generous portion of casserole and passed the bowl to Lizzy. "Let's go back a bit. After our meeting with Chief Elkhurst, we went to search Salamander's room and found some interesting photos. He gave them to Lizzy, who had transferred the bowl to Jason.

She studied the pictures and handed them to Holly. "So, Garcia knew about Mary, obviously." She rolled her eyes.

"Then we went to the hospital to speak with Darla," Jason said. "That was a surprise. She said her visitor was the chief's wife, Marjorie." He looked at Borrego.

"I checked with the next-door neighbor and got confirmation of what she was wearing yesterday. We'll go talk to the chief after dinner."

"Not connected with everything else then?"

"Her son's murder might have acted as a catalyst, but my conjecture is no, it's not related."

"Garcia was on duty this afternoon when he was at the pool. What did Leonard say?" Jason asked.

"It's a long story," Lizzy said. She began with the boat accident and told them his account, up to his assertion that he didn't kill Sal and was with his wife at the time of death. "Could you check the evidence logs at the station and find out if any drugs have gone missing in the last two years?"

"We can put in a request with the chief when we talk to him," Borrego said. "Are you about done eating, Schneider?"

"Yup." He stood. "You two stick together, okay?"

"We will," Lizzy said.

"Do we have dessert?" she asked Holly after they left.

"Of course. But first, tell me what's going on in that devious mind of yours. I can tell you're about to involve me in something Jason wouldn't approve of."

"Are you up for it?"

"Now that he's here, I'm all in." Holly giggled.

"Good. What's for dessert?"

"Ice cream. Now tell me."

"We need to go to Leonard's house and get his journal. No one's home and he gave me the security code."

"So, it's not illegal because he gave you permission."

"Right. But he doesn't want Garcia to know, so we have to be sneaky."

Borrego and Jason sat across from the chief in his office. He offered them coffee then asked, "What's all this about?"

They had agreed it was a touchy subject and discussed how to approach him. Jason was relieved Borrego was doing the talking.

"When Darla regained consciousness she told us the last thing she remembered was your wife's visit.

"This is her statement, if you'd like to read it."

Chief Elkhurst took the thin sheaf of papers and adjusted his readers on the end of his nose. When he finished reading, he placed the statement on the desk in front of him and frowned. "You've heard of a rock and a hard place? That's a featherbed compared to where I'm sitting. What do I even do about this?"

"I can handle it," Borrego said. "But I wanted to let you know and hear anything you might have to add."

The chief ran a hand over his sparse hair and sighed. "Marjorie is one of them women who is sugar and spice on the outside and solid steel on the inside. She's been all cut up by Salamander's death. Wants someone to blame. But what I can't figure is how she knew about Darla and the fifth wheel. I mean, she might have suspected I was having an affair, but somebody must have filled her in, or she wouldn't have showed up at the campground. You get my meaning?"

"Who all knew? Town this size, it's hard to keep a secret."

"I would have said nobody until Salamander took them photos."

Borrego nodded. "We'll go interview your wife now. Darla hasn't said anything about pressing charges, but we'll need a statement."

"I understand. Thanks for giving me a heads up."

"One more thing, Chief," Jason said. He explained their suspicions and asked him to look into the evidence room logs.

Heading to the Elkhurst home, Jason said, "He didn't seem very surprised, did he?"

"Mostly exhausted. A possible symptom of trying to juggle more than one woman." The edges of Borrego's mouth turned upward, not quite a smile, perhaps an acknowledgement of the absurdity of the chief's situation.

At the house, Jason knocked with a feeling of deja'vu. Marjorie answered, not expecting them that time.

"Hello officers. Did you forget something?"

"No, ma'am," Borrego said politely. "We'd like to have a word. May we come in?"

"Certainly. Make yourselves at home. Would you like refreshments?"

"No, thank you." He scanned the cluttered living room and sat in a plush recliner.

Jason sat in another, leaving room for Marjorie on the couch.

Once she was seated, Borrego said, "Darla Gross regained consciousness and made a statement about your visit to the campground. We'd like to hear your version of events."

"She's alive?" Marjorie clamped her mouth shut then began again. "I don't know her, but my hairdresser said…" She glanced at Jason, then at Borrego.

Jason could almost see the wheels turning.

She went on the defensive. "I don't know what she told you, but she tried to kill me. I struck her in self-defense."

"Why were you there?" Borrego asked.

"She asked me to go. I thought it was strange because I didn't know her."

"So she invited you over, and you drove all the way out to the campground."

"Yes."

"Then what happened?"

"She let me in and started accusing me of all kinds of things."

"Like what?"

Marjorie thought for a moment. "She accused me of killing my son and framing my husband. She said I was evil and vindictive." She wrung her hands, and a tear slid slowly down her cheek. Jason was fascinated by her performance.

"Where was the dog?" Borrego asked.

"It was running around barking."

"Darla was making dinner, is that correct?"

She glanced from one to the other again and shifted her weight on the couch. "She was chopping vegetables, and she came at me with the knife."

"You must have been very frightened. What did you do?"

"I grabbed a rolling pin off the table and swung it at her. Then she fell and hit her head on the counter."

"And after that?"

"I was scared. I thought she might be dead, so I ran."

"You didn't call an ambulance."

"No, I told you. I thought she was dead."

Borrego pondered her words for a moment.

"Darla said the stove was on. She was sautéing vegetables. Did you turn it off?"

"Yes."

"What happened to the knife?"

"The knife?"

"You said she was holding a knife. Where did it go?"

"I—I don't know."

"She also told us the pan she was using fell when you hit her. She was worried the dog would get burned. But when we arrived, a clean pan sat on the stovetop and the knife was laying on the cutting board."

Marjorie opened her mouth, then shut it again.

"Are you left-handed?"

"Yes."

"What really happened is you hit Darla from behind. She fell back and hit her head, pulling the pan off the stove as she did so. You took the time to turn off the stove and clean up the pan and the oil; I imagine the dog helped with the vegetables since she was hungry. What I don't understand is why you left the rolling pin."

The calculating look was gone. She tilted her head, face blank. "I don't know. There was so much noise."

"Can you tell me about it?"

Her shoulders slumped and she sobbed. "I've been so upset. My son is dead. My husband doesn't love me anymore. I am alone. When Marty told me about Darla and the fifth wheel I had to see for myself. She's so young and pretty. She was busy trying to get food made and not paying much attention to me. I asked questions and walked around the camper, noticing some of my husband's things, framed pictures of the two of them, and something broke inside of me. I wanted to hurt her."

Mascara running down her cheeks, she said, "I didn't mean to kill her. I swear. When she fell, I panicked; and when I panic, I clean. It's what I do. I focused on the mess and forgot about the rolling pin. I felt powerless and disoriented, and the dog was making it worse. The barking." She grabbed her head in her hands. "I hate little dogs."

"You didn't touch the body?"

"No. I blocked it out. I focused on the mess. My husband will be so angry. Do I have to go to jail since she didn't die?"

"Why don't we take a little ride to the hospital first?" Borrego said gently.

Chapter 26

Defying Death

Lizzy drove Jason's Kia along the winding road to Leonard's cabin. "I'm glad I'm not driving. It's so dark," Holly said.

"I think we're almost there. He said the only turn's the one into his driveway, so keep an eye out."

"Here. It's right here." Mavis squirmed in her lap, trying to see out the window.

Lizzy stopped and backed up a few yards. *No sign of the house, but it must be this one.* She turned right and slowly drove up the gravel road. It wound between trees and ended on a broad, flat expanse of grassland.

Dressed in all black, they sat in the car for a moment surveying the property. The cabin Leonard had referred to was much larger than Lizzy expected. It glowed under the bright moon, the windows reflecting enough light to see, even without a flashlight.

Next to the cabin loomed a barn of equal circumference, but much taller. *Why the barn? Is it a working ranch?*

There was no movement. No light other than the moon. "Ready?" Lizzy asked.

"Let's do this." Holly got out with Mavis and quietly closed the passenger door.

An owl hooted and Mavis barked, making Lizzy jump.

"Just an owl." Holly giggled.

Lizzy shushed the little dog and tiptoed to the front door. She entered the code and stepped inside. The alarm panel blinked. She input the same code, and a recorded voice said, *'House unarmed.'* Holly shut the door behind them.

"Where's the office?" Lizzy whispered.

"Why are we whispering?"

"I don't know. Just in case? Help me find the office.

The cabin was mostly open floorplan with a kitchen on one side and three closed doors on the other. Leonard's office was behind the door at the front of the house, with a window overlooking the gravel drive. Lizzy found the journal where Leonard said it would be and opened it, using a flashlight to examine the entries. "Perfect," she said, then looked outside when she heard tires on the gravel. Headlights shone directly at the window, and she extinguished her flashlight.

"Holly?" she called. "Someone's here."

Colliding with her as she left the office, Holly asked, "What now?"

"Take this and hide in one of the bedrooms. If you're discovered, conceal the book. It's important."

"What about Mavis?"

"There's no hiding her. It might be nothing, but if something happens to me you need to call Jason."

There was a knock on the door and a voice hollered, "Open up. I know you're in there."

Mavis began to bark, and Lizzy opened the door.

"What are you doing here?"

"I might ask you the same question."

"I'm not fooling around. I'm a relative. Why are you here?"

Considering what she should tell him, she paused. "It's none of your business, but I have the security code. Leonard asked me to come."

"So now you're best friends with Leonard. Are you here alone?"

"Well, Mavis is with me."

"Let's take a little walk." He grasped her elbow and propelled her outside. "Leave the dog in the house."

Holly texted Jason. "We need help."

"Where are you?"

"At Leonard's house." She gave him directions. "Garcia showed up and took Lizzy somewhere."

"Are you safe?"

"He doesn't know I'm here."

"Stay put. We're on our way."

Holly had a hard time staying hidden. She wanted to know where Garcia took Lizzy and if she was okay. But she knew if he found her, they would have a bigger problem. Crawling to the living room window on her hands and knees, she lifted her head just enough to see the porch and part of the driveway. Mavis was in a frenzy, barking and throwing herself at the door.

As Holly watched, Garcia walked through her field of vision and disappeared. She heard an engine and the crunch of gravel. *Jason said to stay put, but he's gone, right?*

She opened her phone and sent another text. "He left. There's only one road, so you'll pass him on your way here."

"Is Lizzy with him?"

"No. Can I go look for her?"

"Wait a few minutes to make sure he doesn't return. We'll be there soon."

Holly closed her text app and watched the clock. After two minutes, she slowly opened the front door and peeked out. Mavis raced by her, straight to the barn that sat to the left of the house. Not very good with distances, she thought it might be about five yards away, not far in any case.

She's in the barn. "Lizzy?" Holly put her ear against one of the large doors, trying to hear over Mavis' barking. *What is that?* She realized the Kia was missing.

Did he leave the car running in there? "Lizzy!" she called more loudly, pounding on the door. Panic rising, she examined the heavy chain and key lock holding the doors closed. *Is that the only way in?* She jogged the circumference, then hid in the shadows as a car approached.

Filled with relief, she bent over with her hands on her knees when she saw Jason and Borrego exit the vehicle.

Jason ran toward her. "Where's Lizzy?"

"I think she's in there. I can't get inside. And listen."

Jason put his ear against the barn doors. "Is that the Kia? How long has she been in there?"

"I'm not sure. Since before I texted you he left."

<hr>

Jason went into problem-solving mode. "Do you have bolt cutters, Borrego?"

"No. I have a tire iron."

"I'm afraid that won't do it. Maybe the windows? Give me a boost." The barn had windows, but they were a long way up. Borrego squatted beneath one of them so Jason could stand on his shoulders, then slowly stood. Jason reached his arms up until he could grasp the edge of the sill and, muscles straining, pulled himself up to where he could see inside.

The interior was dark, lit only by moonlight. He cupped his hands around his eyes and waited for them to adjust. He saw the car first, then Lizzy's blonde hair glowing in the moonlight. He would have missed her in her black clothing. *She looks so fragile and small.* "Down," he shouted.

Borrego bent his knees too quickly and Jason fell in the dirt, knocking the ranger over as well. "She appears unconscious. Tied to a pole. And the Kia's inside with the engine running. We don't have much time."

"If you break the window with the tire iron, can you get to the ground without killing yourself?"

"It looks like there's a hay loft against the back wall. Why don't we try it over there?"

Borrego ran to his car and opened the trunk, returning with the tire iron and sprinting toward the back of the barn with Jason. "Ready?"

"As I'll ever be."

They went through the procedure again, Jason lifting the heavy metal tool to break the window, taking care to remove as much of the sharp glass as possible. He put on the lightweight gloves he always carried in his back pocket. *Not great, but better than nothing.* "Okay. Here goes."

He could feel the glass cutting into his flesh as he pulled himself up and wiggled through the broken window. After a four-foot drop, his fall was cushioned by hay. He stood and walked along the loft until he found a ladder. Once he reached ground level, he sprinted to the car and turned off the ignition. He ran to Lizzy and shook her shoulder. "Wake up," he said urgently.

No response. He steeled himself against the encroaching panic. *Please be okay. Please be okay.*

In the background, Mavis' barking had been such a constant that he had stopped hearing her until she quieted. He glanced around and saw her watching him. Waiting.

"How did you get in here?"

She started to bark again, running toward a door in the back, under the loft. She returned to him and ran to the door again. He stood and followed her. Inside the door, tools of every kind covered the shelves and walls. He spied bolt cutters in their midst and quickly grabbed them, racing back to the ladder. "Thanks, Mavis," he shouted over his shoulder as he scaled the ladder to the loft. Borrego hadn't remained below the window, so he pulled out his phone and called.

"Where are you? I'm dropping bolt cutters out the window where I went in. Get those doors open."

"Coming."

He dropped the cutters and went back down to the tool room for something to cut Lizzy loose. Scissors wouldn't do. *A knife, maybe? A saw?* He found a large knife that looked sharp and returned to her, noticing the blood for the first time. Mavis stood next to her, nudging her arm and whining. Jason knelt by the pole and used the knife to cut through the thick ropes. Banging outside indicated Borrego was also hard at work and by the time the doors opened, Lizzy was freed. Jason lifted her in his arms and ran for the fresh air.

"Should I call for an ambulance?" Holly asked, staring over his shoulder.

"I can get her there faster."

Lizzy's eyes fluttered open and rested on Holly. "Thanks," she said before they closed again.

"What about Garcia? Did he see you?"

"I don't think so. We pulled over and turned off the lights until he passed. Maybe Ranger Borrego can drive you and Mavis home. We'll figure out what to do about Garcia once we know Lizzy's okay. Call and warn them we're coming."

Mavis didn't want to leave Lizzy, but she wouldn't be allowed in the hospital. Jason backed the Kia out of the barn, placed Lizzy on the back seat, and waved out the window as he drove down the mountain at a breakneck speed.

Chapter 27

Heard it Through the Grapevine

At the emergency room entrance, a nurse and a doctor were waiting with a gurney. They whisked Lizzy away, leaving Jason to provide details to an orderly. When he was finally led to her cubicle, he found her awake with an oxygen tube in her nose. Despite the bandages adorning her head and wrists, she looked in good spirits, smiling as he entered.

"How are you feeling?" he asked.

"I might've felt better. What happened?"

Jason told her about Holly's texts and the difficulty they had getting into the barn.

"Holly still has the book, right?"

"She gave it to Borrego."

"Why aren't they here?"

"We had two cars and Mavis. I imagine they'll be along pretty soon, if you get admitted. Otherwise, I'll drive you back to the motor home and you can see them there."

"There's not much wrong with me. They just wanted to make sure I didn't have any bad effects from the carbon monoxide. What about you? Why do you have blood all over you?"

"Long story. I had to crawl through a broken window."

"Is Mavis okay?"

"Holly will make sure of it." Jason took her hand in his. "You're going to give me an aneurism one of these days. Couldn't you just point and make someone else do the dangerous stuff?"

"I really never mean to do anything dangerous. Leonard said the house was empty and gave me the security code. The house is in the middle of nowhere. Why would anyone drive out there?"

Her brow furrowed. "Unless he told someone we'd be there."

"That concerns me. I'm going to visit him now and find out. Will you be okay here for a while?"

"Yes, I'll just take a little nap."

Upstairs, Jason knocked on Leonard's door and pushed it open. Leonard and the tiny white-haired woman sitting by his bed looked toward the door in surprise. "I'm sorry to intrude. I'm Jason Schneider, Holly's brother."

The elderly woman smiled. "I'm Helene. We've heard a lot about you."

"Leonard's grandmother, right?"

"I'm actually his great-grandmother but who's counting?"

"Could I speak with Leonard privately for a few minutes? If you don't mind?"

She looked at her watch. "That's fine. It's after visiting hours anyway. I'll see you in the morning, dear."

When Helene stood, Jason felt like a giant and Leonard's grin told him he knew what he was thinking. Once she left, he said, "What's up?"

"You sent Lizzy to your house to retrieve a journal," Jason said.

"Did she get it?"

"Yes. Did you really want her to have it?"

Leonard nodded. "I've made up my mind. I want out."

"Someone else showed up and tried to harm her. She's in the emergency room now. Who did you tell she would be there?"

"Just Gran. Will she be okay?"

"Yes. She'll be fine."

"I shouldn't have sent her."

"Could someone have overheard your conversation with Helene?"

"I suppose so. My wife is staying with her, and she tells Frank everything."

"Did Lizzy tell you about Mary and Frank?"

"No. Are they okay?"

Jason wondered what or how much he should say. *Would I want to know if it were me? Would I want proof? Once seen, that can't be unseen.*

"When Lizzy and Holly went to the pool earlier, they saw Mary and Frank skinny dipping. Then Borrego and I stopped by and found them doing a lot more than that."

Leonard struggled to sit up. "Not Mary. She wouldn't do that to me."

"I have video evidence, but I thought you'd prefer not to have that stuck in your head."

"That's the only way I'll ever believe it. After all we've been through. And Frank's her *cousin*."

"First cousin?"

"I'm not sure. That family is complicated. But still, does it matter?"

"Mm, technically maybe."

"Show me." Leonard held out his hand.

Pulling up the video, Jason gave him the phone and cringed.

He was a brawny, tough-looking guy but as he watched, his face twisted, and his eyes became suspiciously moist. Jason wished he hadn't shown him.

They sat together in silence after the recording ended, Leonard staring at nothing, Jason giving him space.

"Part of me wishes I hadn't seen that," Leonard said, his voice flat. "But I never would have believed it otherwise. That kind of betrayal. I wouldn't have thought it of her."

Ranger Salsbury knocked and peeked her head into the room.

"Could you give us another minute, Ranger?"

She popped back out and closed the door.

"Now I'm wondering if anything was real.

"Did she really lose her memory? Did she know about the drugs? Was it just about the insurance?"

"I was thinking about that too," Jason said. "If you were to die, and Mary was presumed dead, who would the insurance money pass to?"

"I'm not sure anyone would get it."

"Do you have a will?"

"No."

"How about your grandmother? Do you know if she has a will?"

"I'm sure she does. She's always very prepared."

"Do you know who inherits when she dies?"

Leonard stared at him with raised eyebrows. "You think it's about money."

Alone in her ER cubicle, Lizzy thought about everything that had happened since their arrival in Texas. *Before we went to Leonard's, I thought I had it all figured out. Now I have no idea.*

First she thought about Sal's murder. Her abductor could have killed him without any suspicion. Then, the seeker. Yep. The hit and run. Ditto. She already knew about Darla. What she didn't know was why. *Maybe Sal was murdered because of the blackmail but why did he try to run me down? I didn't know anything. And again tonight. I guess this time the reasoning was clearer. He didn't want me to get the journal. But how did he know I'd be there? Did Leonard tell him?*

Jason returned. "Would you like to stay here tonight or go back to the campground?" he asked.

"I want to go back."

"Good. They'll bring the discharge paperwork in a few minutes."

"You already knew." She grinned.

"It was an educated guess."

"What did Leonard say?"

"He didn't tell anyone except his grandmother, but someone might have overheard. Do you think Helene has a lot of money?"

"That's subjective. How much is a lot? I would say she's definitely comfortable."

"I was wondering if it was enough to kill for."

"Why don't we go talk to her tomorrow? It's too late to go now."

"Holly texted and said to hurry."

Lizzy laughed. "Tell her to have the s'mores ready."

By the time Lizzy got discharged and Jason drove her back to the motor home it was the middle of the night, and she might as well have stayed at the hospital. Ranger Borrego was asleep on the sofa, his sock feet up on the coffee table and his hat tipped down over his eyes. Mavis lay next to him with her head in his lap. Holly was in the loft bed, snoring softly. Mavis' head went up and the barking began. "Shh," Lizzy told her, but the damage was done. Borrego was immediately alert, and Holly looked over the side of the loft.

"About time," she said with a big yawn.

"I'll go now and pick up the evidence logs in the morning," Borrego said.

"Take the journal too so you can look at it before you come over," Jason said. "Mavis will be up at six, but some of us might want to sleep in." He elbowed Lizzy.

"I can always dream," she said. "Where are the s'mores?"

"You don't need s'mores," Holly said. "Go to bed."

Borrego moved toward the door.

"Thanks for staying with me, Nelson," Holly said.

"You're welcome," he mumbled. "See you in the morning."

"Where should I sleep?" Jason asked, after Borrego left.

"You take the bedroom. I'll sleep out here with Mavis."

Lizzy folded the table up and unfolded the stuffed benches into a bed.

"I can sleep out here."

"I don't think it's long enough for you. I'll be fine." She watched him walk toward the bedroom, then pulled a pillow and sheet out of one of the benches. She didn't really mind sleeping in the dining room, but it occurred to her that she didn't have her toothbrush or her pajamas. "Come on, Mavis. Let's get some sleep."

Chapter 28

Money as a Motive

The morning chaos was bewildering. Mavis' barking woke him. Jason lay in the enormous king-sized bed and listened. Lizzy and Holly discussed breakfast. The RV's door opened and closed. The clatter of pans in the kitchen. The smell of coffee. *Ahh blessed coffee.* Jason sat up and looked at the clock on his phone. *Six o'clock. It's going to be a long day.*

After he dressed, he left the bedroom and found his sister in the kitchen area. "Coffee?" she asked.

"Yes, please. I heard you talking about breakfast. What did you decide on?"

"We didn't." She giggled. "Any requests?"

"What can you cook in here?"

"Anything."

"Pancakes and bacon?"

"Coming up." Holly began retrieving ingredients from the pantry and the refrigerator.

"Did you bring everything from your own kitchen?"

"Most of it. Plus, we went shopping. We might be running low on a few things. Why don't you take Lizzy's coffee outside? I'll have this ready in about twenty minutes."

Jason set one cup on the counter then opened the door. Holding it open with his foot, he said, "Lizzy. Help," and handed her a cup when she grabbed the door.

She resumed her seat next to a small campfire and took a sip. "The mornings are lovely," she said.

"The weather is great too. I didn't expect it to be this warm."

"I think I should be a snowbird."

"That would be cheating."

"What time will Borrego be here?"

"He didn't say. I could text him and ask."

"No need." Holly disembarked with Candy and her own coffee. "He's on his way. We can eat as soon as he gets here." She put the kitten in the pen with Mavis and sat on one of the logs. "What's on today's agenda?"

Lizzy stood as Borrego pulled his vehicle to a stop. Her stomach growled like a grizzly. "Foo-ood!" she yelled. Mavis howled along with her.

"What's going on?" Borrego asked.

"Lizzy's having a food frenzy. We'd better eat." Holly giggled and led them back inside. "I've only cooked four because I didn't want them all to get cold." She heated the pan and poured more batter before placing four pancakes and a plate of bacon on the table.

Lizzy snagged a piece of bacon on her way to the refrigerator, where she pulled out the apple sauce, syrup, and a bowl of berries. "Who wants more coffee?" Three hands went up.

After Lizzy had eaten several pancakes, she took Holly's place by the stove so she could eat. Borrego was beginning to loosen up a little. He even smiled a couple of times. When she ran out of batter, Lizzy resumed her seat and took another piece of bacon, glancing down at Mavis' pathetic whine. "I bet you think we don't feed her," she said to Borrego.

"I can almost guarantee she wouldn't be that chubby if you didn't."

"Got that right." Lizzy stood. "I'll make some more coffee. Jason, why don't you tell Ranger Borrego about the money."

"Money?"

"Yeah, I was talking to Leonard last night and the subject came up." Jason reiterated the conversation. "The life insurance, the drugs, possible family money. We need to find out who stands to benefit from what. Lizzy suggested we go see Helene this morning."

Borrego nodded. "I'd like you to take a look at what I found. These are the confiscated drugs that were logged into the evidence locker. I highlighted the ones that correspond to Leonard's journal."

Jason studied the list. "Has anyone checked the locker to see if they're missing?"

"I sent the highlighted list back to the chief and he said he'll check personally."

"Let's go interview Helene." Jason stood. "Then we can stop by the station."

Borrego nodded and stood as well. "Thank you for breakfast. Home cooked food is a real treat."

Corporal Quirk answered Helene's door with a frown. Jason thought the square black frames of his glasses were somehow at odds with his round head. Borrego asked if they could speak to Helene, who could be seen sitting on the couch. The Great Dane by her side sat obediently, watchful.

"Of course," Quirk said, backing slightly. "Are you up for company, Gran?"

"Yes, dear." She stood. "Come on in. Is that Jason?"

"Yes, ma'am, and Ranger Borrego."

"I knew you were a ranger. I saw you at Marjorie's the other day."

Borrego removed his hat. "Nice to meet you, ma'am. We'd like to speak with you in private if we may."

"Of course. Marty's on his way to work, I believe. Would you like coffee?"

"No, thank you. We just had breakfast."

"You have a good day, Marty. I'll see you later."

Thus dismissed, Quirk nodded and reluctantly let himself out, looking back with a frown as he shut the door.

"That was good timing. He was starting to badger me, and I didn't know how to get rid of him without hurting his feelings."

"What was he badgering you about?" Jason asked.

Helene's fathomless black eyes seemed to look right into his soul. "Have you ever had someone you cared about, who was just bad to the core?"

"Yes," he said quietly, thinking of Pearl Rice."

"Marty was jealous of Salamander and has somehow decided I'll be changing my will now that he's gone. It makes me wonder."

"That's what we wanted to ask you about too," Borrego said. "Do you have a large estate?"

"Well, now, I reckon I do. My husband was a wealthy man and I'm what you might call frugal."

"Your will is recent, I presume?"

"Absolutely. All of my worldly possessions are to be divided among my children, grandchildren, and great grandchildren. There aren't as many left as you'd think, but each of them will get a substantial nest egg."

"Was Sal included in your will?"

"I was thinking of leaving him the house, but he made it clear he wanted to leave town for good. So no, he wasn't."

"Where's Mary?" Jason asked.

"She went to see Leonard. I told her it was a bad idea."

"Was she in the room when you spoke to him last night?"

"No. Marty was over, and they don't get on."

"I believe that's all we needed to know." Borrego stood. "Thank you for your assistance."

"Ranger? There's one more thing. I wasn't sure I should give it to you, but I've made up my mind." Helene stood and crossed the room to an ornate secretaire next to the fireplace. She opened a small drawer and pulled out an envelope. "These are Salamander's final snapshots. He left them with a friend. Y'all should have them." She walked back and placed the envelope in his hand.

Chapter 29

He Shot Himself in the Foot

The photos Helene gave Borrego showed Marty Quirk passing something to Leonard at the keg party. Jason was confused. "I thought Garcia was passing the drugs. Are they in it together?"

"We're going to have to talk to Leonard again but first let's go see what the chief's come up with."

Officer Mills was attending the front desk when they arrived at the station. She was a serious-looking young woman with a pencil stuck in her small, tightly wound bun.

"Good morning," Borrego said. "We're looking for Chief Elkhurst."

"He's expecting you. Take that hall and turn left."

They heard the banging before they saw him. He was sweating profusely and swearing under his breath.

Borrego knocked on the counter and said, "Mornin' Chief."

The chief stopped what he was doing and mopped his forehead with a large handkerchief. "They're all missing. Not signed out; just gone. It goes back almost exactly two years. Do you know who's responsible?"

"We will by this evening. I'll need a report documenting your findings."

"This'll be the end of my career."

"Not necessarily. You've identified a problem, and we'll work together to find a solution. Right now, our top priority is to put the perpetrator behind bars."

"What's your next step?"

"We'll be at the hospital, interviewing Leonard."

181

Lizzy wanted to walk back to the lake.

"Are you going to bring your gun?" Holly asked.

"You're always telling me not to." Lizzy chuckled. "How about I bring the TASER?"

"Will that stop someone with a gun?"

"As long as it's not pointed at me. Did you make sandwiches?"

"Give me a sec. You should probably wear long pants. I remember all the bandages last time."

"Hopefully this time I won't have to crawl home in the dark."

"I suppose you have a point."

"Ready to go for a walk, puppy?" Mavis wagged her tail. "Are you bringing Candy?"

"Might as well. She's been cooped up here quite a bit."

By the time Lizzy put harnesses on both animals and filled water bottles, Holly was ready to go. They took the direct route to the lake, which was much quicker than the first time, and turned right to follow the shoreline. When they approached the entrance to the clearing where they found Sal's body, Mavis strained against her harness.

"She wants to keep going," Lizzy said.

"Let's see where she's headed."

Mavis trotted forward along the path then took a sharp left into the bushes.

"Oh no, I should have worn the long pants."

The little dog stopped and barked. Lizzy tripped over her and kicked something hard.

"Oww." She looked down. "It's a dirt bike."

"How did you know it was here?"

"Aroherer," Mavis said, looking proud of herself.

"Do you think it's Sal's?" Holly asked.

"More than likely. Text Jason while I look through the saddle bags." She hunted through the one on top, but the other was laying under the bike so once Holly had sent the text she said, "Help me lift this."

"Mavis, cut it out."

Together they lifted the bike high enough to pull the saddle bag out from underneath. Lizzy gave Mavis' leash to Holly and was about to open the bag when a branch snapped and a voice said, "Stop right where you are."

Lizzy looked up, into the barrel of a gun. Holding his weapon with two hands, Marty Quirk stood, eyes narrowed behind square black glasses. *That's what's different. What happened to his glasses?* Then she remembered the broken glass at the crime scene and everything fell into place.

"I'm glad you're here. We found Sal's bike," Holly said.

Quirk seemed to think that was funny. "You didn't tell her?"

"Tell me what?"

Lizzy slowly reached her hand into her pocket and thought she'd better keep him talking. "She was there. I thought she saw you."

"Amazing how one policeman looks like another in uniform." He smirked. He dropped his left hand and lowered the gun to his side. Lizzy took her chance.

In one swift movement, she raised the TASER, holding it with both hands, and pressed the button. The wires flew forward and hit his chest. His large muscles convulsed. His middle finger spasmed on the trigger of his gun and he shot himself in the foot.

Holly stared wide-eyed as Lizzy kicked the gun away from his hand and picked it up. "You only have thirty seconds. Take the animals and run."

"I won't leave you."

"Go. He'll be really mad when it stops."

Jason and Borrego sprinted toward them and Lizzy exhaled with a whoosh.

She handed Jason the gun and stepped back as Borrego cuffed Quirk.

"Why didn't you arrest him last night? If I'd known he was lurking around I wouldn't have brought Holly out here."

Jason stared at her. "Why would we have arrested him?"

"For trying to kill me?"

"It was him? Holly said it was Garcia."

"My foot," Quirk groaned.

"He shot himself," Lizzy explained. "And yes, it was him."

"But why?"

Lizzy opened the freed saddle bag and felt around inside, drawing out a photo of Quirk and Leonard. "The missing piece." She handed it to Jason.

"Let's get him to the hospital and you can explain everything," Borrego said. To Quirk, he said, "You'll have to walk a little way."

<hr>

They all ended up in Leonard's room. After the doctor tended to Quirk's foot, they were joined by Helene, Mary, Garcia, and the chief.

Quirk sat on the bed that had been Darla's. Mary, Garcia, Helene, and Holly sat on folding chairs.

"Why's Quirk handcuffed?" The chief asked.

"Why don't you start, Lizzy?" Jason said.

She looked around the crowded room. "Well, I'm not sure where to begin. I noticed the first clue before I knew it was a clue. Quirk and Garcia came to the motor home after we reported a break in. It took them three hours to respond, probably because they were busy at the party down the road."

"Hey now, wait a minute." Garcia stood.

Lizzy's eyebrows rose. "Everyone knows you were there. We saw the photographs."

He slowly sank back onto his chair.

"When Holly and I first met Quirk, he was wearing unusual glasses, noticeable, with frameless lenses except for a solid black frame across the top. We commented on them after he left. At Sal's murder scene, he looked different, but I couldn't quite pinpoint why. Even though he was speaking in the same know-it-all tone, his movements didn't seem as sure. He was stumbling in the sand and seemed to have trouble with the camera. I took pictures at the scene and noticed later that his uniform shirt was baggy, and he wasn't wearing his glasses. The following day he was wearing square glasses with a solid black frame. The ones he's wearing now."

"So? I broke them. It happens."

"Where did you break them?"

"I don't remember."

Lizzy raised her eyebrows. "The next incident was when I accidentally ended up at the lake at dusk without a flashlight. I texted Holly before my phone died and she called Garcia."

"What's that have to do with it?" Garcia asked.

"You and Quirk went to find me. Did you stay together the whole time?"

"No, we split up so we could search faster."

"I told Holly exactly where I was. Who went there?"

"Quirk. He told me to start further down."

Corporal Quirk pulled at his handcuffs and tried to stand, but the pain in his foot stopped him.

"My dog led me to the clearing and dug up an earring and some pieces of broken glass. I was hiding in the trees when someone else showed up, searching for something. Mavis wouldn't be quiet, so I let her off the leash."

Lizzy watched Quirk carefully. "You were looking for your broken lens, weren't you? And you hurt Mavis. What did you do to her?"

"I have no idea what you're talking about. Garcia found the dog."

"No I didn't. You pointed her out and made me pick her up. She was really mad."

Quirk shrugged. "Who cares. We found your dog for you. You should be grateful."

"I couldn't figure out why you came back for her. Why didn't you just leave her?"

"You can't even prove it was me. If it was, I would have left her there."

"No, I think you decided that by *finding* Mavis, you'd prove that you were really trying to rescue me."

"Why else would I be out looking for you?"

Everyone in the room watched the conversation unfold like a ping pong match.

Finally losing patience, Quirk said, "Even if your ridiculous story was true, why would I kill Sally? He was just a dumb kid."

"Not exactly a kid. A twenty-five-year-old man your grandmother adored and might have left an inheritance. A young man who had aspirations of becoming a paparazzi and who happened to be out taking pictures the night of the party."

"So what?" Quirk snapped. "Let him take his stupid pictures."

"The pictures he took of you passing drugs to Leonard, along with Leonard's testimony and the missing drugs from the evidence locker will put you away for a long time."

"A bunch of lies." Quirk glowered at her. "Why are you letting her go on and on?" he asked the chief.

"Why did he try to run over you? It was him, right?" Leonard asked.

"As you all know, Sal accidentally photographed a lot of people doing things they shouldn't have been doing. He needed money to move out of his parents' house, so he decided to try his hand at blackmail."

"I begged him not to," Helene said. "I told him he should burn those snapshots."

"The morning of his death, he made contact with several of his victims, including Quirk. He showed them his photographs and assured them he had copies. When Holly gave Quirk and Garcia the ones we got from Helene, the picture of him passing drugs wasn't there. He assumed Holly and I had kept it and knew too much. So, he had Holly arrested and tried to hit me with the Jeep. Then he searched the motor home."

"I should sue you for slander." Quirk growled.

"Who gave the order for Holly's arrest?" Borrego crossed his arms.

"I did, based on Quirk's report," the chief said.

"She was placed in a cell without food or water for two days. We'll have to address that in the near future."

Chief Elkhurst began to sputter. "I didn't know. Is Quirk responsible for that too?"

"He is, but as the chief, especially of such a small precinct, you should be aware of everything that goes on in your station."

Lizzy forged ahead. "What got me confused was Leonard's use of the word cousin. He spoke of Garcia and his cousin in a way that seemed interchangeable, and I misunderstood. When he sent me to his house to find his journal, I thought we were finding evidence against Garcia. But you were talking about Quirk, weren't you?"

Leonard nodded. "He found Mary and he was blackmailing me. Everything is in the journal."

"You'll be sorry, you double crosser," Quirk snarled at him.

"I don't think so. I might be charged with selling your drugs, but I can't do it anymore. And I contacted the insurance company and explained what happened. They agreed not to press charges if I return the money."

"Are you out of your mind?" Mary yelled. "After all you put me through?"

"You don't care about me. You can rise from the dead and enjoy your life with Frank."

Garcia's face turned an interesting shade of purple.

"We're getting a little off track here," Borrego said.

"Right," Lizzy said. "Quirk made another attempt on my life, and I saw his face. There was no mistake. Holly, however, was hiding inside the house. She didn't see his face, just the uniform and the cruiser. She texted Jason and Ranger Borrego that it was Garcia, because that's what I thought when we went to the house."

"I can't believe you thought I was a murderer," Garcia said.

"I'm sorry, Lizzy. Quirk didn't even cross my mind," Holly said.

"Other than the weird change of glasses, I didn't really pay any attention to him either, until he drug me to the barn and knocked me out. And I assumed afterwards that he had been arrested. Otherwise, I would never have suggested taking a hike. There we were, minding our own business, and suddenly he shows up with a gun."

"Lucky you took the TASER." Holly grinned.

"Not so lucky for me," Quirk mumbled.

Ranger Borrego crossed his arms. "The final piece of the puzzle was the photo Helene gave us, the same one Salamander had in his saddle bag."

He glanced at Lizzy. "Do you still have the broken glass you found?"

"Yes, and the earring. I thought it might belong to Darla because she said she lost one, but Quirk was just throwing evidence like mud to see what would stick. Emiliano's boots, the chief's uniform shirt, the earring."

"This is all your fault." Quirk glared at Lizzy. "If you hadn't come here, Sally wouldn't have been out taking pictures. I wouldn't have broken my glasses, and I wouldn't have had to do all that other stuff."

"I agree," Mary said. "If you hadn't come, Leonard wouldn't have found out about Frank and me, and he wouldn't have given all the money back."

Lizzy canted her head. "Didn't you say you hated having to hide out?"

"Sure, but we're talking *millions*. What would you do for five million dollars?"

Lizzy silently pondered the question. No one had paid her to leave the public eye and hide out in Harperstown.

Chapter 30

The Dust Settles

Chief Elkhurst and Ranger Borrego transported Quirk to the station. Frank and Mary drifted off without saying goodbye. Helene sat by Leonard's bed and took his hand.

"When you're released, you'll come to me. I have plenty of room and can help while you recover."

"Thanks, Gran. I'm sorry about everything."

"I guess it keeps life interesting, but I'll sure miss Salamander. He's the only one who took time for me."

"I'll visit more. I got so caught up trying to please Mary that I let everything else slide." He gave a harsh laugh. "And there she was canoodling with her cousin."

"You were right, you know," he said, looking at Jason. "They were trying to figure out how to get more money from me if I died. I'm…" He shook his head. "Gutted."

"We should probably go," Lizzy said. "I'm exhausted."

"I imagine you'll be leaving Serenity soon. Why don't you come to my house for dinner tomorrow night? I feel like we should celebrate an evening of normalcy before you go," Helene said.

"That sounds lovely." Holly and Jason nodded their assent. "What time should we arrive?"

"How about six?"

"We'll be there."

The three of them left the hospital and returned to the campground. To Lizzy, it felt like an eternity since she and Holly had set out on their hike, but it was just past lunchtime. "I'm hungry," she said.

"Let's have a proper cookout. I'll make burgers," Jason said.

"I'll make salad," Holly said.

"I'll lay in the hammock and drink a beer."

They laughed.

Mavis was overjoyed when they got back. "I'm not going to put her in the pen," Lizzy said. "If Jason's cooking burgers, she won't be going anywhere."

"True. And Candy will go wherever Mavis goes."

Lizzy sat on a camp chair and watched Jason as he got the fire started. "What happened to the chief's wife?"

"When she finally admitted to what happened, she sounded like she might be mentally unstable, so Borrego took her to the hospital for a psychiatric evaluation. Apparently he was right. They've sent her to the state hospital for treatment."

"Do you ever think about cause and effect?" Lizzy asked. "Like, does a traumatic event cause a psychotic break, or do the symptoms of psychosis end up causing the trauma?"

"Maybe neither." Jason shrugged. He watched the fire for a moment, then sat on the log across from Lizzy. "You've solved the murder case." He put up a finger and grinned. "Don't say it. It was you, not Mavis. You and Holly are free to go. Are you still heading for Los Angeles?"

"Holly should probably be here for this conversation."

"Did I hear my name?" She emerged from the RV with a plate of raw burgers and gave them to her brother.

"You did. Jason was asking about LA."

"Can we still make it?"

"Possibly. Just. But I've realized I'm not ready. I thought I was, but I need more time. When I think about driving out there, every part of me screams NO."

"What about the speaking engagement?" Holly asked.

"Kirk knew I wasn't ready. He had a backup all along. I argued with him, but he wasn't fooled. You brought it up too." Lizzy smiled.

"I'm pretty sure you wouldn't have even considered going if you hadn't beent trying to pull me out of my funk."

"But it backfired, and you want to go home. You can fly back with Jason if you want."

"I thought perhaps we could trade places," Jason said. He didn't meet her eyes, concentrating instead on placing the burgers on the grill.

Silence.

Holly recovered first. "I'll fly home if Jason stays. You shouldn't travel all that way by yourself."

"Is that what you want?"

Holly nodded.

"Well, I guess we're travel buddies," Lizzy told Jason. She stood. "Anyone else want a beer?"

⸻ ❦ ⸻

Jason watched Lizzy enter the motor home. "Why are you staring at me?" he asked his sister. "Was that a bad idea?"

"Why would you think that?"

"She didn't look very enthusiastic."

"I don't really understand what's going on between you two. As far as I can see, you're perfect for each other, but…" She scrunched her face. "Why don't you want to be together?"

"I don't think it's as simple as that. It's kind of like the trip to Los Angeles. She's not ready. And her friendship is really important to me. I don't want to lose her because I'm impatient."

"I see. I think."

Lizzy returned and Holly excused herself to finish the salad.

Mavis watched Jason flip the burgers and whined.

"Did I overstep? Would you rather I didn't travel with you?" he asked.

"It's not that. We always have fun together. It was just un-expected."

"We can take our time and explore on the way back, maybe ride horses or go fishing. I haven't had a proper vacation in years."

"That does sound fun. Hurry those burgers. I'm starving."

"Aurhouerer."

"Mavis too." Lizzy stretched out on the hammock and closed her eyes.

She looks so peaceful. I wonder what she's thinking about. He had no doubt she had something going on in that active brain of hers.

Ranger Borrego arrived about the time the burgers were ready and agreed to join them for lunch. He preferred his burger well done, as did Holly. Jason thought the two of them were well-suited, but he didn't mention it because he didn't want Holly to move away, and Barker would have his head. Well, not literally, but he'd certainly be unhappy. He liked Barker and respected him, but he and Holly were both easy going. Jason suspected he didn't need her the way Borrego might. She made him smile and perhaps lightened the heavy burdens he carried. Jason sighed. *Not my business.*

They ate inside because the flies were annoying. Lizzy pulled sriracha ketchup and jalapenos out of the refrigerator, sharing them with Borrego. He also enjoyed great piles of onions. Holly made a face and Jason chuckled.

"What happened at the station?" he asked.

"Quirk finally confessed. Lizzy got everything right. He was jealous of Sal and concerned about his inheritance. The blackmail was the last straw. Sal had become a liability."

"What happened to Sal's camera?" Lizzy asked.

"He said he threw it in the lake. I've got divers out looking for it now."

"Will Lizzy need to return for the trial?"

"I doubt it. Since he's confessed, a comprehensive statement will probably do. That's why I came over, actually. I typed one out from my notes, but you'll want to go over it and make sure it's correct before you sign it. I made one for Holly as well." He smiled at her.

"Did Helene invite you to supper tomorrow?"

"Yes. She was still at the hospital when I went over to speak with Leonard."

"What's going to happen to him?" Lizzy asked.

"I spoke to the superintendent and the District Attorney, and they agreed that based on the circumstances and his willingness to cooperate they'll drop the charges against him. He's provided enough evidence to convict Quirk of stealing the drugs and coercing him into selling them. His testimony and Sal's photos provide the motive for murder."

"I'm glad he'll be okay. He was in a very bad situation."

After dinner, Lizzy asked if they could have s'mores.

"What is it with you and s'mores?" Holly asked.

"I never had them before. I'm pretty sure they might be my new favorite food."

"And I'm pretty sure everything you eat is your new favorite food." Holly giggled.

Lizzy appeared to consider that before she said, "No. I don't like Brussel sprouts… or liver."

Holly stared at her for a moment, then got up and opened the pantry.

Chapter 31

Dinner Party at Helene's

On their last night in Serenity, Lizzy, flanked by Jason and Holly, rang Helene's doorbell and waited. Every light in the house was lit and country music played loud enough to hear from the front porch. When she opened the door, the elderly woman looked younger, more vibrant. Not that she looked sixty, Lizzy thought, but she certainly looked as though a weight had been lifted from her shoulders. She greeted them and invited them inside.

To the right of the entrance, the front room furniture had been pushed against the walls, leaving ample space for socializing. The fireplace at the far end of the room blazed merrily and guests stood in small groups, chatting and laughing.

To the left of the entrance, a twenty-person dining table gleamed beneath an ornate chandelier. The wooden table was set with fine China, cloth napkins, and candles. "Do you need any help with dinner?"

Helene smiled. "Thank you for asking, but I hired a caterer. It would have been too much for me. Go ahead and get yourselves cocktails and say hello to everyone." She wandered off to speak to a man Lizzy didn't know.

"Can I get you a drink?" Jason asked. "She's hired a bartender too."

Lizzy looked past him at a temporary bar in the central hall. "See if he can make a Long Island iced tea."

"That sounds good. See if he can make two," Holly said.

"Are you sure?"

"Are you still doing that big brother thing?"

"Sorry. On my way."

Holly giggled as he walked away.

Scrutinizing the other guests, Lizzy realized she didn't know everyone present.

"There's Darla. Who's she talking to?"

"I don't know. Let's find out." Lizzy strode toward the two women and said hello."

"Hi, Lizzy. I hear you're leaving tomorrow."

"Yes. We've been here a lot longer than we intended."

"Have you met Sal's friend Patricia?"

"No. Nice to meet you." She looked around for Holly, who had stopped to speak to Ranger Borrego.

Helene rang a little bell and announced dinner. "Find your place cards and we'll do introductions."

Once everyone was seated Helene sat at the head of the table and smiled. "Thank you all for coming. It's been a long time since we've all dined together. This is a special occasion because everyone here was involved in Salamander's murder investigation in one way or another and because four people who helped solve the case will be leaving Serenity in the morning. If you haven't met them, let me introduce you to Lizzy and Holly, who've been staying at the campground, and also Ranger Borrego and Holly's brother Jason, a police captain from South Dakota." She indicated each of them as she said their names.

"Here's our first course."

A server entered the dining room with a tureen of soup. "Cold Gazpacho," he announced. He moved around the table, stopping to ladle soup into the bowls of anyone who said they'd like some.

When he left, Helene took a bite of soup. "Correct me if I'm wrong, Ranger, but I believe the reason the murderer was so hard to identify was because every suspect was hiding something. I felt guilty about Sal because I knew something was off with the police department but couldn't figure out what it was. I wanted to warn him; I *did* warn him, but I couldn't tell him *who*."

Borrego put his spoon down. "Plenty of secrets in this town. Perhaps you could introduce us to your guests who weren't in Sal's photos."

"Certainly."

The server entered again with Waldorf salad and a crisp white wine.

Helene introduced the mayor, Coach Gross, and Art, explaining her investigative activities the day she met Lizzy and Holly. Then she introduced Patricia and her mother, Darla.

"Thank you, Patricia," Borrego said. "The photos Sal left with you were the proof we needed to convict Corporal Quirk of selling confiscated drugs."

"I wish we didn't have to talk about this while we eat," Mary said.

The look Helene gave her was acrimonious. "You can leave if you want. This dinner is a goodbye to you too. I embraced you as my granddaughter-in-law and you betrayed Leonard and me. This will be the last time you're welcome in this house."

Mary opened her mouth to respond, to argue perhaps, but Garcia interrupted her. "I think we should leave." He stood and held out his hand.

She stood as well. "You shouldn't always side with him. He's not perfect you know."

"He's family and he's never done anything to hurt you."

Garcia pulled Mary from the room and the server returned with steak and pasta, paired with a rich cabernet sauvignon.

The food was delicious. Seated between Darla and the mayor, Lizzy hoped the courses would stop before she reached capacity. She didn't want to miss a bite.

She looked across the table at Holly and Borrego, who had their heads close together and looked like they were discussing something engrossing.

They're a good fit. I wonder if they've noticed it themselves. Then she thought about Barker and felt guilty.

Helene sank into quietness after Mary and Frank left. Jason, seated to the elderly woman's right, was watching Lizzy. Their eyes met and he gave her an enigmatic smile. *He can see it too.*

With her final sip of Moscato, following a decadent chocolate mousse, Lizzy leaned back in her chair with her hands splayed across her stomach. "Helene, you should ask the chef to come in here and accept the laud he or she deserves. It's been a long time since I had such a wonderful meal."

"I'll see if he's still here." She went into the kitchen and returned with Emiliano.

The day Lizzy found the boot was the last time she had seen him. Her mind went blank as she tried to recall some long-forgotten Spanish phrases.

Borrego beat her to it. "Muchas gracias, señor. Hace mucho que hemos comido una cena tan rica."

With a little bow, Emiliano said, "Gracias. Me alegra que Ustedes la disfrutaron."

"Deliciosa," Lizzy said belatedly, wishing she had kept up with the language she had studied so many years ago. Having been raised in Arizona, there was really no excuse.

Emiliano gave her a brief nod, looking somewhat amused. He looked at Helene. "Okay now?"

"Yes, thank you so much."

The room was silent for a moment after he left.

"That was awkward," Lizzy said. "Thank you for saving the day."

"I do what I can." Borrego gave one of his rare smiles.

"I have one more little treat for you," Helene said. "The bar is still open, and I've hired a DJ. Dancing in the living room." She stood and led the way.

Several hours later, the guests had thinned and most of those who remained collapsed on the sofas and chairs lining the wall.

Holly and Borrego danced to a slow song and Jason handed Lizzy a glass of water. "Good thing we don't have to leave super early," he said.

"Mavis will have me up at six anyway."

"Don't you ever go back to bed?"

"No, once I'm up, I'm up."

"We could just drive an hour or two after we drop Holly off. You know, take it easy."

"Or we could make Borrego take her to the airport and just stay here."

"You wouldn't mind?"

"I like it here. Now that the bad guy's locked up. Maybe we could even go for a swim, if I can get the image of Frank and Mary out of my head."

Jason chuckled.

Helene approached and sat next to Lizzy. Taking her hand, she said, "I wish you were going to stay. My life is going to be very different now."

"You could come with us." Lizzy smiled. "I bet you would love my neighbor, Mrs. Fickle."

"I'm afraid I still have responsibilities here, but perhaps you'll allow me to visit sometime."

"That would be wonderful!" Lizzy looked around. "Where's Lucky?"

"He's taking a nap upstairs. He's well trained, but he's bigger than me and if he gets over stimulated, I can't control him at all."

"There's something to be said for small dogs, although Mavis can be pretty stubborn."

Helene turned her focus to Jason. "Could you tell me if anything's to be done about the police department? We can't leave it the way it is."

"Yes, Ranger Borrego will be assisting."

She gave a little nod and stood. "I'm glad to hear it."

After she moved away, Lizzy asked, "Does he have a plan?"

"They'll bring in an interim chief and begin internal investigations. I imagine it will be a time-consuming process but like Helene said, they can't just leave things the way they are."

Chapter 32

Saying Goodbye

They didn't have to ask. Ranger Borrego volunteered to take Holly to the airport the next day. He arrived early for breakfast. Holly had outdone herself. Lizzy eyed the fruit salad, waffles, eggs, bacon, fried potatoes, and toast laid out on the table and her stomach growled loudly.

Mavis sat alert. "Arooherer."

"I know, right? This is like Christmas morning without the peppermint."

Holly giggled. "True. I should have brought some."

Lizzy smiled. As the only person in her family who didn't like the Harperstown tradition of everything peppermint at Christmas, it was perfectly understandable that Holly hadn't brought any with her. "Not necessary. This is amazing."

By the time they finished, not a scrap was left. "I'll wash the dishes so you two can say goodbye," Jason volunteered.

"I'll help," Borrego said.

"Thanks." Lizzy grinned. "Let's take a little walk."

Holly followed her out the door and they walked around the corner toward the party site. "Are you upset that I'm flying home early?"

"No. I understand. It won't be the same without you though. Are you taking Candy with you?"

"Yes. They said I could take her in the cabin with me, since her carrier is so small."

"Are you looking forward to seeing Barker?"

Holly looked at Lizzy in surprise. "Of course."

Staring straight ahead, Lizzy said, "I thought maybe you and Borrego had some kind of connection."

"Well, we do… but that doesn't mean I don't care about Barker."

"I didn't mean that."

"It's funny how I've been single all these years and then I suddenly find two wonderful men. Not funny really. Odd. They are both great."

"I think Borrego suits you better, but he lives far away. It wouldn't be convenient. Did you tell him about Barker?"

"Yes. He asked if he could visit. We decided to just wait and see what life throws at us."

Lizzy drew her house key out of her pocket. "The construction's probably not done on your house, so stay in mine for now."

"You'll only be gone for a few days, right?"

"I'm not sure. Jason's been talking about taking our time and exploring on the way back and I rented the motor home for a month. I'll let you know."

"I kind of wish I was going with you now." Holly said.

"You still could."

"No, I want to go home. This week has been really traumatic. I want to feel like everything is back to normal. It would help if my house was ready."

Lizzy stopped and gave her a hug. "I know what you mean. Why don't we head back? They're probably done with the dishes."

Holly linked arms with her, and they began the walk back. "Have you figured out what you're going to write next?"

"Yes, actually. I have."

"Well? Don't keep me in suspense."

"It's a historical mystery, set in the old west. I first thought of it when we did that mystery maze. I wanted a church-related crime, but I was focusing on my series and couldn't figure out how to connect them. Since we've been here I've gathered several great character ideas and I'll be able to add a pastor like I wanted."

"What about Rachel?"

"That series can wait. I have a story in my head that needs to be told."

*Be the lovely who
Kindly leaves a review*

Thank you so much for reading.

Booksellers may purchase multiple copies of this book at a discount from IngramSpark.

Mother of two, cat mom, and prolific reader, Alice Kanaka is the author of ten mystery novels, numerous short stories, and a twelve-episode collaboration with Black Knight, author of the *Starshatter* space opera series.

Alice holds a bachelor's degree in Spanish and a Master of Business Administration with a concentration in Human Resources. She spent twelve years working at a state psychiatric hospital, speaks three languages, and has lived in seven countries.

A life-long fan of the mystery genre, Alice's books combine traditional tropes with contemporary characters to create whodunits that are simultaneously familiar and unique. Her aspiration is to write books that she would enjoy reading; stories that are both entertaining and uplifting, perfect with a cup of Earl Grey and a roaring fire on a gloomy day.

HTTPS://AliceKanaka.com